G000067874

THE SANDY BAY COZY MYSTERY SERIES

AMBER CREWES

PEN-N-A-PAD PUBLISHING

THE SANDY BAY COZY MYSTERY SERIES

BOOKS 7-9

GINGERBREAD AND SCARY ENDINGS

ABOUT GINGERBREAD AND SCARY ENDINGS

Released: October, 2018
Series: Book 7 – Sandy Bay Cozy Mystery Series
Standalone: Yes
Cliff-hanger: No

Business is good but the stress of fulfilling a new corporate order is almost driving Meghan Truman insane. She is therefore excited when handsome detective, Jack Irvin, proposes to take her to the movies. She never expected that a fun, carefree night at the Sandy Bay cinema would end with the tragic death of the movie theater manager.

Who would stand to gain from his demise?

As Meghan delves deeper into this murder investigation, she discovers that stress has a way of bringing out the worst in people. With the clock ticking to find the murderer, will she be prepared when a serendipitous act of kindness puts her squarely in the path of a killer on the loose?

1

Everyone has their favorite season. Meghan Truman's was fall. She delighted in gazing at the red, orange and brown leaves that adorned the trees coupled with the weather being not too hot and not too cold. This was the perfect recipe for snuggly nights indoors, watching popular TV shows and indulging in yummy treats. There was so much she was thankful for in her life. She had settled into her adopted hometown, Sandy Bay, and had a thriving business and good friends. Perhaps, above all, she was glad about her stable relationship with Jack Irvin, a local detective who had proven his love for her on numerous occasions. Even though he had a busy schedule, it seemed he always made time to surprise her with visits at her bakery. That morning as she prepared for the day, she was glad to spend some quality time with him before things got busy.

"I just think it would be a good idea to take a break, Meghan."

Meghan Truman's heart sank as she turned to face him. "What did you say?" Meghan whispered incredulously as she stared in Jack's blue eyes. "You want to take a break? I thought our relationship was going well, Jack! I know things were a little tense when I was in Paris last month, but everything has been back to normal since I got home."

Jack burst out laughing as Meghan looked at him in horror. "This is not a time for laughing, Jack," she exclaimed as Jack reached over and pulled her into his strong, muscled arms. "First you tell me we need to take a break, and now, you're hugging me?"

Jack shook his head as he planted a kiss on Meghan's cheek. "Meghan," he said patiently. "You weren't listening. You have been so preoccupied with this new corporate order that you hardly hear anything I say, sweetheart."

Meghan pushed Jack away and raised an eyebrow in confusion. "What are you talking about?"

Jack smiled, showing his deep dimples. "I was saying that it would be a good idea to take a break from your *work*, Meghan. Not our relationship. You've been working nonstop at the bakery since you received that massive corporate order from the Behzad Corporation, and I'm worried that you are going to work yourself to death!"

Meghan sighed in relief, wiping a bead of sweat from her forehead as she tried to slow her racing heart. Jack was *right*; Meghan's bakery, Truly Sweet, had received a large corporate order that had been keeping Meghan and Trudy, her trusted assistant, busier than they had ever been. Meghan was grateful for the business; Behzad Corporation was one of the largest manufacturing businesses in the Pacific Northwest, and Meghan knew a professional relationship with the company would be invaluable. Meghan also knew, however, that she was near her breaking point; she had been working nearly twenty hours each day, and she was exhausted trying to fulfill the large order.

"I thought it would be fun to take a break and go to the

movies," Jack explained as he drew her close. "We haven't had a date night in forever, and I think it would be fun!"

Meghan pursed her lips as she thought of the hundreds of cupcakes, croissants, donuts, and eclairs she still needed to make; she had several hours of work to finish, and Meghan knew that it would be impossible to fulfill her obligations *and* have fun.

"Don't you dare say no!" she heard Trudy yell from the kitchen. "Meghan Truman, get out of this bakery right now; you need a break, and I will stay up all night baking if it means you get to have some fun."

Meghan felt her eyes brim with tears as Trudy marched into the dining area of the bakery. "You are too sweet, Trudy," Meghan said as she wrapped her arms around Trudy. "You are the best assistant a girl could ask for." Both ladies started laughing as Jack did a victory dance around the bakery, pumping his fists in delight. Meghan glanced up at the large, red antique clock in the middle of the bakery and was glad to know there would be enough time for her to have a quick shower and change into something nice for her date night.

Two hours later, Jack and Meghan walked hand-in-hand into the Sandy Bay Cinema. After purchasing their tickets, Jack directed Meghan to the concession stand. "The Sandy Bay Cinema makes the best gingerbread in the world!" Jack declared as he bought two gingerbread cookies. "You have no idea."

Meghan laughed. "The Sandy Bay Cinema sells *gingerbread*? That is so random."

Jack grinned as he popped a piece of his cookie into his mouth. "Random, but I'm not complaining," he chuckled as he wiped the crumbs from his lips.

"Stop that!"

Meghan and Jack turned to see Mrs. Sally Sheridan, one of Sandy Bay's elderly residents, hobbling across the Sandy

Bay Cinema lobby. Mrs. Sheridan was like black licorice; you either loved her or wanted to run two hundred mile per hour in the opposite direction when you saw her coming. After several unforgettable interactions with Mrs. Sheridan, Meghan was definitely not a fan. Mrs. Sheridan's mouth was agape, and she waved her cane up and down as she moved closer to Meghan and Jack.

"Put that gingerbread down, Jack Irvin!" Mrs. Sheridan screamed as she raised her cane above her head, bringing it down to strike Jack's hand, knocking the remainder of his gingerbread cookie out of his hand.

Meghan placed a hand over her mouth in shock. "What are you doing, Mrs. Sheridan?"

Jack shook the hand that had been struck, wincing in pain. "Mrs. Sheridan," he warned. "Mrs. Sheridan, I am off-duty right now, but as a Sandy Bay Detective, I have the authority to take you in to the police station after hitting me with your cane. What on Earth were you thinking?"

Mrs. Sheridan shook her head. "Gingerbread is bad luck, Jack Irvin. I don't care if you are a detective or a clown; you should know that gingerbread is bad luck, and you shouldn't be eating it."

Meghan's dark eyes widened. "Mrs. Sheridan, I've never heard anything like that before."

Mrs. Sheridan bit her bottom lip and howled as Jack defiantly stuffed another piece of gingerbread into his mouth. "Don't let him do that," she pleaded with Meghan. "Gingerbread is bad luck, and you two are going to be sorry."

An attendant walked up to the trio. "Is everything okay?"

Meghan smiled politely. "I think we're fine. We are just going to head into our movie. I think Mrs. Sheridan could use some help getting to her seat, if you wouldn't mind?"

Mrs. Sheridan glared at Meghan and Jack as the attendant took her by the elbow and led her into the closest theater.

"Well, that was a horror movie!" Meghan exclaimed as she turned to look at Jack. "Good thing we're going to that silly comedy; I think I've had *enough* drama today."

Jack shrugged his shoulders. "Sweetheart, I didn't realize you wanted to see the comedy," he began. "I really wanted to see the new horror movie…"

Meghan sighed. "It's alright," she told Jack. "I really don't like horror movies, but you *did* get me out of the bakery tonight. I'll be fine. Apart from a scary ending, I think I can just about manage to enjoy any movie I see as long as good prevails over evil. What's the worst that could happen in a horror movie, anyway?"

2

"I can't hear what they're saying, Jack," Meghan whispered as Mrs. Sheridan wailed for what felt like the millionth time since the movie began. "Mrs. Sheridan has been screaming through the entire movie. I have no idea what's going on in the plot."

Jack yawned, reaching over to tuck his arm around Meghan. "Sorry, I closed my eyes for a moment," he admitted as a redheaded woman yelled on screen. "What's going on?"

Meghan clenched her teeth, annoyed that she had agreed to see the horror film and now had no idea what was even going on. "I don't know," she hissed to Jack as the actress fainted at the sight of the serial killer. "Mrs. Sheridan's constant wails, sighs and sobs are robbing me of the opportunity to enjoy this film."

Jack yawned again and rubbed his eyes with his spare hand. "Just relax," he murmured to Meghan as he leaned back in his red leather seat. "It's probably not the best movie ever made, but things could be worse…"

Meghan's heart fluttered as Jack pulled her closer. She breathed in the deep, familiar scent of his cologne, feeling her face grow warm as she leaned in to Jack's embrace. "You're right," Meghan whispered as she happily snuggled closer to Jack. "Things could be worse."

The movie continued, but rather than being annoyed by Mrs. Sheridan's endless screaming, Meghan settled in, thinking about how lucky she was to be enjoying date night with her handsome, loyal boyfriend. Trudy was minding Truly Sweet and preparing the orders for the next morning, and Meghan knew that she had nothing to worry about.

"I can't believe I was fussy earlier," she thought to herself as she watched Jack's eyelids droop. "I'm at the movies, on a date with the most handsome man in all the Pacific Northwest. My wonderful assistant is holding down the fort back at my business. What else could I ask for?"

Meghan's thoughts were interrupted by another piercing scream from Mrs. Sheridan as the killer on screen attacked another unsuspecting victim, but Meghan did not mind; she smiled as she watched Jack's head droop, and she giggled with the realization that he had fallen asleep.

"He's too cute when he is sleeping," she thought as Jack's chest rose and fell. "I've never seen him asleep before. I think my heart might just burst."

Mrs. Sheridan screamed again, and Meghan nearly leaped out of her seat. "I didn't expect that," she whispered as Jack's eyes remained closed. "Her screams sound like they could be from the movie."

Suddenly, there was a loud bang, and Meghan felt her heart pound in her chest as she frantically looked around. She noticed that the other moviegoers appeared to be startled as well, and Meghan leaned over to shake Jack's shoulder.

"Jack," she whispered as his eyelids fluttered. "Jack! Wake up!"

Jack stirred and slowly opened his blue eyes. "What? What did I miss?"

Meghan's dark eyes widened. "I just heard a loud noise, Jack."

Jack shook his head. "Meghan, it's a horror movie. There are so many noises and screams. I'm sure it's fine."

Meghan bit her bottom lip. "I don't know, Jack," she protested. "Look around. The other people in the theater look scared, too. It isn't just me."

Jack raised an eyebrow. "Meghan," he began. "I'm a Sandy Bay detective, Sweetheart. If something were wrong, I would know it. Trust me. It was probably just a noise from the movie, or maybe Mrs. Sheridan is being a nuisance with that cane of hers. Just relax. I know you've been on edge with your work schedule, but you should try to enjoy our night together, okay?"

Feeling embarrassed, Meghan nodded, leaning back in her seat and softening her shoulders. "Jack is right," she thought as his eyes closed again. "I'm uptight from my hectic work schedule and I need to just take it easy."

Before Meghan could return her attention to the movie screen, the lights in the theater came on. Meghan's jaw dropped as a uniformed attendant marched to the front of the room and began waving her arms up and down.

"Ladies and gentlemen," the attendant yelled. "Ladies and gentlemen, please make your way to the exits on either side of the theater; we are evacuating the building at this time, and we need everyone to leave immediately!"

Meghan rose to her feet and tugged on Jack's arm. "Come on, Jack! Let's get out of here."

Meghan and Jack followed the crowd outside. They all huddled together in the parking lot as the screams of police cars filled the air. Jack pulled out his cell phone and dialed Nunan, the Sandy Bay Police Chief.

"You're kidding me," Jack lamented as Meghan's stomach filled with dread. An ambulance pulled up next to the curb, and a team of EMTs burst out of the doors and dashed into the movie theater. "And you're sure it was a gunshot? Okay, good to know. Since I was here in a personal capacity, I'm sure I'll have to speak to the officers, but as soon as I'm released, I'll be at the station."

Jack hung up the phone and looked down at Meghan. "It's not good, Meghan…"

"What do you mean?" she asked. "What happened, Jack?"

Jack wrinkled his forehead and shook his head. "It's bad. I shouldn't say anything, but since you were in the theater, you'll find out anyway; Tom Doncaster, the manager of the Sandy Bay Cinema, was shot while we were watching the horror film."

Meghan clutched her heart. "Oh no, Jack! That's terrible! Is he alright?"

Jack gestured at the EMTs, who were exiting the movie theater with a large, black bag. "It doesn't look like it," Jack muttered underneath his breath. "Chief Nunan didn't have all the details yet, but from the looks of that body bag…"

Meghan's stomach lurched as she watched the EMTs load the body bag into the back of the ambulance. "That must have been the loud noise I heard during the movie, Jack. It was a gunshot."

Jack's blue eyes widened, and he pulled a notepad out of his back pocket and scribbled down a few lines. "I'm sure the officers will want to talk to you, but as a detective, I need to get that down," he informed Meghan. "Is there anything else you can tell me, Sweetheart?"

Meghan shook her head. "That's all I heard, Jack," she answered softly. "I can't believe it was a real gunshot. What a tragedy."

Meghan nearly jumped out of her skin as she felt a tap on

her shoulder. She turned to find Sally Sheridan grimacing at her, her cane raised.

"I told you kids," Mrs. Sheridan said. "I told you!"

Jack looked over at Mrs. Sheridan, a look of annoyance on his face. "Told us what, Mrs. Sheridan?"

Mrs. Sheridan rolled her eyes. "Did you forget already? I told you kids that gingerbread is bad luck, but no one listens to old Sally Sheridan!"

Meghan pursed her lips. "Mrs. Sheridan, that's terrible."

Mrs. Sheridan wrinkled her nose. "I'm just telling it how it is," she said. "I told you kids that the gingerbread was bad luck, and you ate it anyway. Now that man is dead. His blood is on your hands, Meghan Truman and Jack Irvin, and you two should be ashamed of yourselves!"

3

"You two should be seriously ashamed of yourselves," Mrs. Sheridan continued as Meghan began to cry. "You ate the gingerbread, and you're just as bad as the murderer!"

Jack glared at Mrs. Sheridan. "That is enough," he ordered Mrs. Sheridan as he looked around the parking lot at the chaos that was brewing in the crowd. "Meghan, it looks like people are getting pretty shaken up; I am going to go ahead and go on duty and talk with some witnesses. Will you be okay here?"

Meghan's eyes flew to Mrs. Sheridan's angry face. "Umm…"

Jack gently took Mrs. Sheridan by the elbow. "I'll take the chance to speak with Mrs. Sheridan," he told Meghan as he began to walk away with the elderly woman. "Meghan, you just take some deep breaths and relax; I will try to get us out of here as soon as we can."

Meghan's heart was pounding as she took a seat on the curb. She thought of herself only moments ago in the theater, snuggled up with her boyfriend and enjoying the evening, and her heart ached as she pictured Tom Doncaster being murdered.

Suddenly, Meghan's phone rang. It was Karen Denton, her dearest friend in Sandy Bay. Karen and Meghan had met a few years earlier when the two had lived in Los Angeles; Sandy Bay was Karen's treasured hometown, and after failing to secure a career in acting in Hollywood, Meghan had been convinced by Karen to move to Sandy Bay. Despite their significant age difference, Meghan adored Karen; at seventy-three years old, Karen was the most energetic, spirited woman Meghan had ever met, and Meghan loved her company and counsel as she navigated her new life and new business in Sandy Bay.

"Meghan!" Karen screeched as Meghan answered the phone. "Meghan, are you alright?"

Meghan's hands shook as she gripped the phone, but she nodded. "I'm alright, Karen. Did you hear about what happened at the theater?"

"Oh, sweetie, I did," she cried. "I was leaving the pilates studio when the news came on the television in the lobby. I called you to tell you, and when Trudy told me that you and Jack were at the movies, I could have just died with worry."

Meghan sighed. "I heard the gunshot, I think," she told Karen. "But I'm fine, and so is Jack."

"Thank goodness," she said. "I was so worried about you, sweetie. Meghan, on the television, they said a body was recovered. Do you know who it was?"

Meghan took a long breath. "Tom Doncaster? I don't know him, but Jack said he was the manager?"

Karen shrieked. "Tom? Tom Doncaster? Oh no! She finally did it! She finally did him in!"

"What are you talking about?" Meghan asked Karen. "Who did him in?"

"Everyone around Sandy Bay knows about Sheila

Doncaster," Karen huffed. "Sheila, Tom's wife. She's been madly in love with one of the fitness instructors at my gym for years! Everyone has always seen the way she's treated Tom; she speaks—spoke—to him like a dog, and she was obviously in love with the fitness instructor instead of her husband. Everyone always joked that Sheila would kill Tom someday so that she could run off with her fitness fellow, but I never really believed that she'd get the guts to do it."

Meghan's mouth opened. "Are you serious? Would she really do that?"

"Oh, yes," Karen confirmed. "Sheila Doncaster is a real witch. She was a spoiled little rich girl growing up, and when she married a movie theater manager, everyone was confused. Word on the street was that she married for love, but that she got bored before the ink was dry on their marriage certificate."

"That's terrible," Meghan said as she rose to her feet and began pacing around the crowded parking lot. "I'm going to tell Jack about her."

"You don't need to bother," Karen sighed. "Everyone knows about Sheila and Tom. I'm sure the police have already gone to pick her up. It was only a matter of time...."

Meghan finished her call with Karen and tucked her phone back in her handbag. She took a moment to digest all that Karen had told her. As a teenager growing up in Texas, she had worked at the local cinema and knew the stress some of the managers went through. The job usually involved late nights, and Meghan could see how Sheila Doncaster may have suffered many lonely nights on her own. She was also aware of the inaccuracy of the Sandy Bay rumor mill, as she had been the target of it on a few occasions. Being a small town, it seemed everyone knew everyone else's business. Meghan was initially amazed at how fast news traveled around town when she first arrived in Sandy Bay, but after having lived there for a while, she was used to it. She didn't condone it, but could see why Sheila might have been tempted to find solace in the arms of another man who wasn't her husband. But to kill him? Something just didn't feel right about that and she hoped she'd be able to get to the bottom of this murder mystery.

4

There are some days you never want to end because you're having so much fun. Today was not one of those days for Meghan Truman. She couldn't remember having such a night where things had started so well but ended up miserably.

"That was not the relaxing date night I wanted to give you," Jack lamented as he pulled up in front of the bakery. "I'm so sorry, Meghan."

Meghan shoved a stray piece of dark, wavy hair out of her eyes as Jack came around to open the passenger door for her. She took his hand as he helped her out of the car, and leaned into his tall, muscled frame as he walked her to the front door.

"I just wanted you to have some fun," Jack apologized. "I didn't expect Tom to be shot, or that Mrs. Sheridan would go bananas on you."

Meghan rolled her eyes at Mrs. Sheridan's name; after Meghan had ended her conversation with Karen, Mrs. Sheridan came back to torment Meghan, and had not stopped until Jack threatened to arrest her. Mrs. Sheridan had been placed in the back of a squad car, and Meghan was interviewed by Chief Nunan, along with two other Sandy Bay Police officers.

"It wasn't the date night I was hoping for," Meghan admitted as she and Jack stood in front of the bakery door. "But I'm glad we got to spend some time together."

Jack smiled down at Meghan and put his strong arms around her waist. A shiver flew up her spine as he pulled her close, and she closed her eyes, tilting her chin up as Jack kissed her softly on the lips.

"Thank you for coming with me," Jack whispered as he gently pulled away and kissed Meghan on the forehead. "And thanks for being patient with me while I was on-duty; you are a trooper, Meghan Truman. A real trooper."

Meghan felt butterflies in her stomach as she watched Jack walk back to his car; he was so tall and good-looking that Meghan still felt nervous every time she looked into his eyes. She had hoped for so long that they would start dating, and now that he was her boyfriend, Meghan could not have imagined a better Prince Charming.

"Tonight was scary," Meghan thought to herself as she stepped into the bakery and greeted Fiesta and Siesta, her two little dogs. "But having Jack there was really nice; I feel so safe with him, and he knew just how to handle Mrs. Sheridan when she was bothering me. I just hope he can solve this murder quickly; there's a killer on the loose in Sandy Bay."

The next morning, as Meghan finished arranging a dozen freshly made donuts in the front display case, she heard the familiar chime of the little silver bells attached to the front door of the bakery. Meghan tucked her hair behind her ears and smiled as a familiar looking adolescent boy shuffled into Truly Sweet.

"Good morning!" Meghan chirped as the boy blushed. "What can I do for you today?"

The boy raised an eyebrow at Meghan. "Miss Truman, don't you remember me? I'm Danny. From the movie theater?"

Meghan nodded, remembering her brief encounter with Danny after the movie theater had been evacuated. He had been taking tickets at the outdoor ticket booth during the murder, and Jack had hastily interviewed him as Meghan watched nearby.

"Your boyfriend grilled me in the parking lot; he's a scary guy, that Detective Irvin." he exclaimed, as he bent down to study the variety of donuts in the display case. "I've never talked to the cops before; I'm a straight-A student and an Eagle Scout, and I had no idea what to say or how to act."

Meghan smiled warmly at him. He was tall and skinny, and he moved awkwardly like all teenage boys do. She remembered seeing the terrified look on his face as Jack questioned him in the parking lot, and she gestured at the donut case as he licked his lips. "Those are fresh, you know," she said kindly.

"Great. I'm in charge of taking in breakfast for the swim team this morning, and I thought donuts would be a good pick. The team will be so excited to have some fresh treats for after our workout."

Meghan bent down to slide the display case open. "What sounds good to you?"

He furrowed his brow. "Let's see... how about fifteen jelly-filled and fifteen glazed? Oh! And thirty donut-holes, ten lemon, and fifteen chocolate donuts! That should be enough."

Meghan chuckled. "I should hope so."

Danny grinned. "I need the sugar and the fuel, Miss

Truman. Between the swim team, school, and working at the movie theater, I'm pretty busy."

Meghan stared at him as she wrapped each donut in Truly Sweet's signature yellow paper. "You do sound busy. Speaking of the movie theater, how do you like working there?"

He shrugged. "Well, to be honest, it had been tense for a while. Before Tom was killed, him and Lawrence Reid were always going at it. It could get so weird sometimes."

Meghan bit her bottom lip. "Lawrence Reid?"

He bobbed his head up and down. "Yeah, Lawrence Reid. He worked at the movie theater forever. Him and Tom never got along, and they were always fighting. Tom finally fired him last week, and Lawrence was so mad that he egged Tom's car!"

Meghan's jaw dropped. "It sounds like he was pretty angry."

"Oh, he was. But anyway, I'm running late for practice, so I need to get going," Danny informed her as he eyed the clock on the wall.

"The donuts are on the house today," she told him. "Thanks for coming in."

"Thank you, Miss Truman. That is awfully nice of you," he said with a silly wink as he walked out with three cardboard boxes of fresh donuts.

As Meghan giggled at Danny's attempt at being flirtatious, she heard a familiar voice.

"Meghan Truman."

Meghan looked up to see Kayley Kane, a sassy, no-nonsense real estate agent, marching toward the counter on six-inch heels, her lips bright with pink lipstick and her hair loose. "Kayley, how are you?"

Kayley snapped her gum, her eyes bright with excitement. "I can't complain. I might have a new opportunity on the horizon, Meghan. Also, can I get a croissant? I'm dying for something delicious this morning."

Meghan nodded and reached into the display case for a fresh, flaky croissant. "Here you are," Meghan said as she handed the croissant to Kayley. "Anything else?"

Kayley shook her head. "Nope! A sweet treat and some sweet news, all in one morning. Lucky me."

Meghan tilted her head to the side. "What are you talking about, Kayley?"

Kayley leaned across the counter to whisper into Meghan's ear. "The movie theater," she breathed. "Word around town is that it's going to be up for sale. It's going to be a *big* sale, Meghan, and I think my boss is going to let me have it if it comes up…"

Meghan's dark eyes widened. "Kayley," she said slowly. "A man was *murdered* at the theater, and you're already thinking about the *sale?*"

Kayley shrugged. "It's not an ideal situation, but I really, really want to be behind the sale. Anyway, I have to run. Here's a five for the croissant. Keep the tip."

Kayley turned to sashay out of the bakery, and Meghan began twirling a dark, wavy lock of hair between her fingers. "Tom was *murdered*," Meghan thought to herself as she recounted the conversation with Kayley. "And Kayley looked as though she had won the lottery. *Why* is she so excited about that sale? What's in it for Kayley if the theater sells?"

5

The next day, Meghan glided her car into a parking space at the Sandy Bay Farmer's Market. It was a bright, crisp morning, and Meghan smiled as the sunshine warmed her face. She breathed in the heavy, thick scent of the salty sea air, savoring the way it clung to her face and hair as she stepped out of her vehicle.

Meghan scanned the crowd in search of Lawrence Reid, the man Tom Doncaster had fired from the movie theater before Tom had been killed. After mentioning her conversation with Danny to her, Karen had insisted Meghan go to speak with Lawrence.

"I bet he knows something," Karen had declared during their phone call. "Lawrence and I worked together in the local pharmacy many years ago, and he has always been trouble. It's funny how one day, he is fired from his longtime job, and then immediately after, the man who fired him is *dead*."

Meghan had agreed. "You're right. I should talk to him."

"Yes, you should," she said. "His wife runs a stand at the farmer's market every Tuesday. He usually helps her out. I bet you can catch them there tomorrow. Here, I'll text you a picture of him so you know who you are looking for."

When Meghan spotted Lawrence at the farmer's market, her heart sank; he appeared older than the picture Karen had sent her, and his eyes were weary. Meghan slowly ventured over to the booth where Lawrence was sitting, and she leaned down to greet him. "Lawrence Reid?"

Lawrence's eyes flashed with anger, and Meghan felt her stomach churn.

"Who wants to know?"

Meghan shook her head. "You aren't in trouble! I'm Meghan Truman? I own the bakery in town? I just wanted to ask you a few questions…."

Lawrence narrowed his eyes at Meghan. "I know who you are," he hissed. "You're the girlfriend of that detective! Look, lady. I don't know anything about Tom Doncaster's murder. That jerk didn't treat me well, but I sure as heck didn't kill the man."

Meghan placed a hand on Lawrence's shoulder. "I'm not here on my boyfriend's behalf," she said softly. "I was at the movies the night everything happened. I just want to find out who killed Tom."

Lawrence glared at Meghan. "I hate to say it, but that man had it coming."

Meghan's dark eyes widened as she edged away from Lawrence. While he was older, he was a huge man, and Meghan took in the sight of his huge biceps and muscular build as he stared into her eyes. "What do you mean?"

Lawrence sighed. "He fired me because I had been late to work twenty times in the last month. And you know why? My mom has been terribly ill, and my wife and I are the only ones taking care of her. My wife works out of town most days, so I'm the only one my mom has. Tom knew she was sick, and he knew that's why I had been late, and he fired me anyway. You would think twenty-three years of faithful service to that theater would matter for something, but it didn't. Tom had it coming; you don't fire someone for taking care of their mother. He had it coming, and he got killed…"

Meghan frowned. "I'm sorry to hear that. Did you talk to Tom about the details of what was going on with your mom? I can't imagine anyone would be that cruel to fire you because you were being a good son."

Meghan shuddered as Lawrence puffed out his chest and rose to his feet. "Are you calling me a liar? I told Tom everything, and he fired me!"

Meghan leaned away from Lawrence, feeling her body grow cold as she stared up into his furious face. "I'm sorry, I didn't mean…"

"Didn't mean to make me sound like an idiot? Or a fool?" Lawrence screamed as passersby stopped to stare. "I've had enough of this! Tom got what he deserved, and I am not sorry he's dead after how he treated me."

"I'm so sorry," Meghan whispered. "I'm sure this has been a difficult time for you, with your mother being sick and your… change… in employment. I'm going to go now, but it was nice meeting you."

Meghan turned on her heel and sprinted away from Lawrence's booth. She pulled out her cell phone from her little red purse and dialed Jack's work number. "Jack? I have some news."

"News?" he asked. "What about?"

"I just talked to Lawrence Reid. He had been fired from the movie theater right before Tom died. I think he had something to do with it, Jack. He kept saying that Tom had it coming, and his temper was terrifying."

"Meghan," he sighed. "We have a lead of our own we're working on right now. Can I call you back later?"

"A lead? What kind of lead?" Meghan inquired.

"A lead on the getaway car," he explained. "The security cameras outside of the theater have been recovered. A metallic purple car sped away from the movie theater only moments after Tom Doncaster was murdered, and we're trying to figure out just exactly who was behind the wheel…"

6

If there was something that brought joy to Meghan's heart, it was the opportunity to spend time with her dogs and see them happy. She couldn't wait to have children of her own and having her twin dogs was the closest thing she had to exercising her maternal instincts.

"Come on, my loves!" she called out to Fiesta and Siesta as they walked around the block. "It's another sunny day, but the wind from the sea is too strong. We're going to walk in town today!"

The two little dogs barked good-naturedly as Meghan led them around the corner, and Meghan giggled as they wagged their little tails. "Good dogs! You are such good doggies!" she cooed.

She walked the dogs down the main street of town and around the courthouse. Meghan was tired from a long day at the bakery, but happy to be out and about in the fresh air. She wandered aimlessly, lost in her thoughts, and was startled when she heard a deep voice behind her.

"Can I help you with something?"

Meghan turned around and looked up, realizing she was

in front of the movie theater. A short, sandy-haired man squinted his eyes at her, and Meghan extended her hand. "I'm Meghan Truman! Sorry I didn't see you there; I've been enjoying the nice day and didn't even realize anyone was around."

The man laughed. "It's not a problem. I'm Tim Dollar, the new manager of the movie theater. I was sent out here from the New York headquarters to make sure things are in order with the death of Mr. Doncaster. It's a pleasure to meet you."

Meghan smiled warmly. "Welcome to Sandy Bay. It's a nice little town, so I'm sorry such terrible circumstances brought you here…"

Tim shrugged. "That's what happens. It's all part of the job. Anyway, I was out here walking around the property when I saw you and your little dogs. They're too cute."

Meghan grinned. "Thank you, Tim. They are the little loves of my life."

Tim's face fell. "I had to leave my dog back in New York. I hope I can send for him soon."

Meghan gestured at her two dogs. "Well, if you need a fix of some furry friends, you can always borrow mine."

"Hey, are you Tim Dollar?"

Meghan and Tim turned to see Ryan Branson, the owner of the local confectionary shop. Ryan was tall, with curly black hair and a matching beard, and he was smiling as he approached the pair.

"You must be Mr. Branson," Tim said as he reached to shake Ryan's hand. "We've spoken over the phone so much this week that I would recognize your voice anywhere. How are you?"

Ryan nodded. "I'm well," he replied. "Glad to catch you. Welcome to town. Meghan? How are you doing?"

Meghan smiled at Ryan. He was one of her primary suppliers for little candies and sweets to garnish her desserts, and she had always enjoyed his company. "I'm great, Ryan. Just getting to know Sandy Bay's newest resident. It's nice to have a bright spot amidst all the trouble we've had in town lately with Tom Doncaster's death."

Meghan saw Ryan's face darken at the mention of Tom Doncaster. "Tom was a friend of mine," Ryan murmured as Meghan's heart sank. "We grew up together; he always supported my dream of opening the confectionary, and he was the one who recommended my business to the cinema's head office in the first place. I've been supplying the theater with candy for years."

Meghan hung her head and reached for Ryan's arm. She gave it a gentle squeeze. "I'm so sorry to hear that," she whispered to Ryan. "It's terrible to lose friends. I'm sorry for your loss."

Tim nodded, his face sympathetic. "Terribly sorry for your loss, man."

Ryan shrugged and brushed a stray curl from his forehead. "It is what it is," he said. "I wanted to talk with Tim about our continued partnership. I do hope that the theater will continue stocking the candy from my store?"

Tim smiled brightly. "Let's plan on meeting tomorrow morning to talk it through," he answered.

"Sounds great," Ryan replied as he shook Tim's hand. "Tim, Meghan, it was a pleasure."

As Ryan turned to leave, Tim rolled his eyes. "Maybe what this theater needs is change," Tim muttered under his breath. "The New York office sent me here to clean up this mess, and I'm going to do everything it takes to turn this tragedy into a success. A whopping success, mind you."

Meghan raised an eyebrow. "What do you mean?" she asked Tim. "What does Ryan have to do with any of that?"

Tim bit his lip. "I shouldn't be telling you this," he began.

"But you've been such a nice person to talk with, and you seem to just understand things."

"Go on...." she implored as Tim crossed his arms across his chest.

"Let's just say that we will be making some changes to the theater under my management," he explained. "We'll be going in some... different directions. This theater is in shambles, and I will move mountains to fix this disaster, no matter what it takes."

7

Meghan loved occasionally flicking through the local Sandy Bay Chronicle. She liked getting to know more about the town she now called home. She was pleasantly surprised when she once saw a piece about her bakery in it. This glowing article had identified her bakery as a wonderful place for residents of Sandy Bay to meet up and consume the finest treats in all of the Pacific Northwest. That single article had done wonders in attracting a new clientele base to Truly Sweet. That morning as she thumbed through the newspaper which a customer had left, she spotted a headline that caught her attention.

Stress Identified as the Number One Killer Among Young People

The article said that stress brought about by unrealistic expectations in young people due to social and economic pressures, was the number one factor in causing depression and ultimately a shorter life expectancy among young people. The article went on to say that stress could be over-come by maintaining a consistent exercise regime. Meghan closed the newspaper and took some time to analyze how she had been feeling since she had gotten the big Behzad order. She had found herself snapping at Trudy and being short with Jack on a few occasions. "Maybe I need to exercise more," she thought to herself. Just then, her phone rang. It was Karen.

"Hello Sweetie, just wanted to let you know that I'll be swinging by after my class this morning at the gym. Today's bring-your-friend day, but you've rejected my offer so many times that…"

"I'll come."

"What did you say, Sweetie?"

"I said I'll come. I'll change and meet you in the gym's car park in thirty minutes." Meghan hung up and let out a shout of victory. She was determined not to be a negative statistic and bounded up her stairs, after informing Trudy of her intentions, to change into some gym attire.

"Look, I know what I'm talking about," Karen declared as she and Meghan walked into Sandy Babe, the local gym. "I think Lawrence is a shady character, but don't forget about Sheila, Tom's wife! Like I told you, everyone knows Sheila couldn't stand her husband, and I wouldn't be surprised if she had something to do with his death."

Meghan sighed as they signed in at the gym. She glanced around at the dozens of fit, leggings-clad women milling about the lobby, and Meghan was flooded with embarrass-ment. Meghan peered down at herself. Due to the bakery's massive success, she had not had time to exercise much since moving to Sandy Bay, and she felt self-conscious as she stared at the fitness enthusiasts surrounding her.

"Sheila *loves* this class," Karen whispered in Meghan's ear as the doors to the studio opened and the women began to file in. "I'm sure she'll be here. You can get a good look at her, and then maybe we can talk with her in the locker room after class."

Meghan and Karen walked into the studio, and Meghan gasped. The room had bright, unflattering fluorescent lights, and three of the four walls were covered in floor-length mirrors. "You said that I wouldn't feel embarrassed," Meghan hissed as Karen directed them to the front of the room. "This lighting is terrible; every curve of my body is out there for the world to see, and I can't escape my own reflection in all the mirrors."

Karen shook her head. "Once the music starts and we begin the circuits, you'll snap out of it; this is a no-judgement zone, Meghan. Just enjoy the class!"

Meghan frowned, but she took a moment to be grateful that she had a relatively healthy, strong body that would allow her to workout. "Even if I am not perfect, I am healthy and young and happy," Meghan whispered to herself.

"What did you say?" Karen asked as she adjusted her neon-colored sweatband.

"Nothing," she replied.

"Well, if you're interested, look up; Sheila just walked in," Karen murmured.

Meghan looked at the door as a lithe, elegant woman slipped into the room. Sheila was tall and slender, her hair cascading in loose waves down to her narrow waist. "She looks like a princess," Meghan said in awe as Sheila glided to the other side of the room."

"I know," Karen agreed. "Everyone was so confused when Princess Sheila married Tom, the movie manager. It just didn't make sense."

"Hello, everyone!"

Meghan turned to see a brawny, beaming blonde-haired

man march into the room. All the women perked up at his presence, and Meghan could see Sheila appeared to be especially enthralled.

"Welcome to Sandy Babe Circuits, the best calorie-burning, booty-busting class in the Pacific Northwest," the man announced to the crowd. "Do we have anyone new here? Come on, people. If you're new to our bunch, raise your hand tall and proud. Give us a little wave."

Meghan did not raise her hand, but Karen grabbed Meghan's wrist and lifted it into the air. "She's new. This girl is new," Karen announced. "This is Meghan Truman, my friend! She is new to class!"

The instructor smiled at Meghan. "Thank you for letting us know, Karen. Meghan, welcome to the class. This will be a fun, fabulous workout, and we are so happy you are joining us today."

Meghan blushed, embarrassed to have been outed as a new member to the class, but pleased that the instructor was so encouraging. She adjusted her purple leggings and matching headband, ready for the fun that had been promised.

"Alright everyone," the instructor commanded. "Take your places."

Ten minutes into the workout, Meghan was heaving like an overweight hippo; her heart was racing, sweat was pouring from every crevice of her body, and she could no longer feel her feet. Meghan gasped for breath, and she was in too much pain to care that she was making a spectacle of herself.

"Just keep going," Karen urged Meghan as they bent down into a set of squats. "The first time is always the worst, but you look great."

"I... don't... look... great," Meghan choked as she saw her

red-faced reflection in the mirror in front of her. "I look miserable… and I feel miserable!"

Thirty minutes into the workout, Meghan had to take a break; she pulled herself into a tiny ball on the floor, and she was mortified when the handsome instructor walked up beside her. "Up on your feet, girly!"

Meghan shook her head. "I need a rest," she pleaded as the instructor looked at her in disdain. "I feel awful."

The instructor looked at Meghan, and then over to Karen, who looked like she had stepped out of a sports magazine. "Your friend needs some pep in her step, Karen."

Karen was panting, but she had a smile on her face. "I keep telling her to work out with me, but she always says no."

The instructor grimaced. "Looks like she needs to say yes sometimes…"

When the class had finally finished, Meghan could barely walk to the locker room. "That's what you do every week?" Meghan asked Karen in amazement. "That was the hardest workout I've ever done, and I only managed to do half of it."

"I do it five times each week," Karen said nonchalantly. "It keeps me young. Hey, look, Meghan. Sheila is packing up her bag over there. I'll introduce you two."

Karen led Meghan over to the wooden bench where Sheila was loading her dirty luxury workout gear into a satin monogrammed bag. "Sheila? Sheila, so good to see you here. I'm so sorry for your loss," Karen said softly as they approached.

Sheila looked confused. "My loss?"

Meghan raised an eyebrow. "Your husband?"

Sheila laughed. "Oh, yes! My husband. Forgive me; the endorphins from the class just flooded my head. Thank you for the kind words, Karen. And Meghan, so happy you joined the class today."

Meghan smiled. "It was an adventure, that's for sure."

Sheila tossed her wavy hair behind her shoulder. "This class has been my lifeline for years," she admitted as Meghan and Karen leaned in. "My husband worked so much and was hardly ever home at night, and when I used to get lonely, I would come to this class just to have some company."

"*Used* to get lonely?" Meghan pried.

Sheila sighed. "I think we all know what I mean," she admitted. "It hasn't been a secret that a certain instructor here has become very special to me. Do you know Tom couldn't care less when he found out about me and my instructor? Sometimes though, I wonder what would have happened if Tom had been home more. Would I have even wandered into this gym? Would I have caught the eye of my fitness instructor? I don't know, honestly…."

Meghan's stomach churned. She thought of Jack and his busy work schedule; he was often called into the police station in the middle of the night, and sometimes, she didn't hear from him for days at a time. "Its work," Jack would tell Meghan. "Work keeps me on my toes, beautiful!"

Meghan, Sheila, and Karen walked into the lobby of the gym. The blonde instructor walked by the trio and winked at Sheila. Meghan's jaw dropped, but she quickly recovered her composure.

"I can't help how I feel," Sheila said softly as they walked out of the lobby and into the cool evening. "My husband was never home, girls. He was never around. I fell in love at that gym—with myself, with my body, and with my fitness instructor. I wish that things had been different. I wish that poor Tom were still with us. But I can't change the past. And I'm going to live happily in the moment. And that moment is my new life, without my husband, a man who never managed to make his beautiful, bright wife happy. I have no regrets, girls. No regrets in the slightest."

Karen turned to Sheila and stared at her. "No regrets?"

Sheila shrugged. "Everyone in town knows what I have done," she confessed. "And let me just tell you girls something: when a wife is ignored, she has to do what she has to do to find her own happiness again. Let's just say that I did what I had to do."

8

Sheila's cold words about the state of her marriage kept playing on a continuous loop in Meghan's mind. She couldn't imagine things deteriorating to that level in her relationship with Jack. The arrival of her least favorite person in Sandy Bay broke up her musings.

"I told you, Meghan Truman," Mrs. Sheridan screeched as she waved her cane up and down to destroy the arrangement of fresh gingerbread on the counter of Truly Sweet. "Gingerbread is bad luck! You and that Jack had gingerbread at the movies, and Tom Doncaster was killed! How can you bring this bad luck into your bakery at such a time? Shame on you."

Meghan's dark eyes filled with tears as Mrs. Sheridan kicked one of her display cases. The fresh gingerbread cookies fell to the floor and crumbled, and Meghan shrieked. "Please," Meghan pleaded as Mrs. Sheridan raised her cane. "Please, stop! Those cookies were for a new order, Mrs. Sheridan! The customers paid over the phone. I stayed up all night to make that gingerbread!"

Mrs. Sheridan scoffed. "I don't care," she declared to Meghan. "I told you that gingerbread is bad luck, and you went and filled your bakery with GINGERBREAD. It's like you are asking for bad luck to sneak up and bite you on the bottom, Meghan Truman, and I won't stand for it."

Meghan balled her hands into fists, thinking of the sleepless night she had spent preparing the last minute order. "Mrs. Sheridan," she murmured. "You've ruined my order. What else do you want?"

Mrs. Sheridan stared at Meghan. "I want you to understand that gingerbread should not be in this town," she explained to Meghan as her eyes flashed in anger. "Ever since I was a little girl, anytime gingerbread has been around, there has been trouble! You listen to old Mrs. Sheridan, Meghan. I know what I am talking about."

Out of nowhere, there was a loud crash in the kitchen, and Meghan heard Trudy let out a scream.

"Ouch!"

Meghan turned toward the kitchen. "Are you okay?" Meghan called to Trudy.

"I'll be fine," she replied. "Just spilled some cake batter, but I'll clean it up."

Mrs. Sheridan cackled. "I told you," she said to Meghan. "The gingerbread. The gingerbread caused that woman to fall. I told you, Meghan Truman. I told you."

"Told her what?"

Meghan's shoulders dropped in relief as Jack walked into the bakery. "Mrs. Sheridan, are you talking about the gingerbread again?"

Mrs. Sheridan narrowed her eyes at Jack and gestured at the spilled gingerbread on the floor. "I did what I had to do."

Jack gasped. "You did that? Mrs. Sheridan, I am warning you; if you ruin anything from this bakery ever again, I will arrest you."

Mrs. Sheridan rolled her eyes at Jack and hobbled out of the bakery. Meghan collapsed to the floor and began to cry.

"Oh, Meghan," Jack soothed as he bent down to sit with her. "What happened?"

"I was up all night making gingerbread for a last minute order, and then Mrs. Sheridan came in and destroyed it all. She kept saying that gingerbread is cursed, Jack. She ruined the order, and now, there's another mess to clean up in the kitchen. Trudy fell and spilled some cake batter. It just isn't going well today."

Jack leaned over to wrap Meghan in his strong, muscular arms. "It's okay," he whispered to Meghan as he smoothed her messy dark hair. "I'm here. We'll get this squared away, Meghan."

Jack kissed Meghan on the forehead and pulled her to her feet. "Why don't you go take a nap?" Jack suggested. "You look exhausted. Go rest. I'll help Trudy take care of the mess."

Meghan nodded gratefully. "Thank you," she muttered as she wandered upstairs. "Thanks, Jack."

An hour later, Meghan returned to the kitchen with a smile on her face. "I just got off the phone with the client who ordered the gingerbread," she informed Jack. "They said that I can push the order to tomorrow with no issue. Thank goodness. I have time to begin again."

Jack beamed. "That's great, Meghan," he said. "Trudy and I cleaned up the kitchen, and she told me to tell you that she's going to take next week off."

Meghan bobbed her head up and down. "That's fine; I remember she told me that she was going on vacation. Thanks for helping her clean up."

Jack reached for Meghan's hands and stared into her dark eyes. "Something else happened while you were sleeping," he told Meghan. "I received a phone call from Chief Nunan with an update on the case."

Meghan's jaw dropped. "Did they catch the murderer? Do

they know who it was? From talking with Sheila and Lawrence, I wouldn't be surprised if it were one of those two. They seemed so suspicious, Jack."

Jack bit his lip. "They found the owner of the metallic purple car," he explained to Meghan. "The car that was spotted leaving the theater only moments after Tom was murdered.

Meghan clapped a hand over her mouth. "They found the owner of the car? Who is it, Jack?"

Jack furrowed his brow. "It was Trevor Souza," he said.

"Trevor Souza?" Megan asked. "Who is that?"

Jack's blue eyes were somber, and he gripped Meghan's hand. "Trevor Souza is Sheila Doncaster's fitness instructor at Sandy Babes… the one she has had eyes for, Meghan. Trevor Souza owns the car that sped away from the theater only moments after Tom, Sheila's husband, was murdered in cold blood."

9

Friends are the family you get to choose, and Meghan was grateful for the friendships she had made in Sandy Bay. She had had her highs and lows in her short stay in Sandy Bay, but at every point she had been blessed with friends to share those key moments.

"I'm so glad I have you around to help while Trudy is on vacation," Meghan gushed to Karen as they tidied the bakery. "I've loved having you today!"

Karen grinned, licking blue frosting from her fingertips from a batch of cupcakes she had decorated. "It's my pleasure, sweetie," she said to Meghan. "It's just fabulous to help friends, and you know how much I love helping you!"

Both women looked up as the little silver bells attached to the front door chimed. A stout, mousy-haired woman walked in. "Meghan Truman? I'm Felicia Foust. I made the order for the gingerbread?"

Meghan smiled and walked around the counter to shake Felicia's hand. "Pleasure to meet you, Felicia. Thank you for being so flexible about the pickup date for your order. I really appreciate it."

Felicia waved her hand. "No problem! The gingerbread is for a little work party at the end of the week, so it really didn't matter. Thank you so much for taking on the order last minute. I'm so thrilled to find someone in town who makes gingerbread."

Karen winked at Felicia. "You came to the right place, Felicia," she informed the customer. "Meghan is the best. Her sweets are the best in the Pacific Northwest, you'll see."

Karen went to the kitchen to retrieve the order. She returned holding three yellow cardboard boxes. "Here you are."

Felicia opened one of the boxes, her eyes wide with excitement. "These look gorgeous!"

Meghan smiled demurely. "You are too kind."

Felicia shook her head. "Seriously, these look wonderful. I cannot wait to share them."

Felicia paid Meghan, and as she left, Meghan bid Felicia farewell. "Bye, Felicia!" Meghan called out. "At least *someone* in this town appreciates my gingerbread," she muttered as Felicia left.

The little silver bells chimed again, and Kayley Kane strutted into the bakery. "Meghan Truman," she cooed. "Long time no see. I have some treats to pick up, as well as a question for you."

Meghan sighed, but pasted a smile on her face. "I have your treats right here. What did you need to ask me, Kayley?"

Kayley gestured at the door. "I just passed Felicia Foust walking out of here, and she was gushing about the gingerbread you made for her. I've never heard her be so complimentary of anyone before. Meghan, I have a favor. My son is having a birthday party next week and wants a fruit cake. Would you be available to make one? I know that fruit cakes aren't your usual treats to make, but would you make an exception for me? Just this once?"

Before Meghan could respond, Tim Dollar, the new manager of the movie theater, walked into the bakery. "Meghan Truman! Good evening!"

Meghan waved at Tim and then gestured to Kayley. "Tim Dollar, this is Kayley Kane. Kayley is a real estate agent in town."

Kayley stuck her hand out to shake Tim's hand, pumping it vigorously. "Pleasure. What do you do, Mr. Dollar?"

Tim smiled, revealing a deep dimple on his left cheek. "I am the new manager of the movie theater. I just arrived in town from New York. Our headquarters sent me out here to get that place in shape!"

Kayley's face brightened, and she batted her eyelashes at Tim. "The new manager of the movie theater? Oh, it is an absolute *pleasure* to meet you," Kayley breathed. "I have been trying to track you down for days!"

Meghan watched as Tim raised an eyebrow at Kayley. "You've been trying to track me down? Why is that, Mrs. Kane?"

"Ms. Kane," she corrected Tim as she flirtatiously bit her bottom lip. "I'm not married. Anyway, I've been trying to track you down all week. Like Meghan said, I am a local real estate agent at one of the best firms in town. I wanted to ask you a question about the movie theater. Are you planning on selling the theater?"

Tim shook his head. "Absolutely not," he informed Kayley. "Headquarters sent me out to Sandy Bay to fix things, not to sell the business."

Kayley's face fell. "Are you sure? You are sure that the movie theater is not going to sell?"

Tim laughed. "Ms. Kane, I'll be honest with you. I've had my eye on the Sandy Bay branch of our theaters for a long time, and I am thrilled to *finally* be the one in charge now that Tom is out of the way....I mean, *no longer with us.*"

Kayley frowned. "I see. Well, it was nice to meet you. Meghan, I'll talk to you later." Kayley took her sack of treats and stomped out of the bakery.

"What a lovely woman," Tim admitted to Meghan as she stared into his eyes. "Sandy Bay is just filled with the nicest, prettiest girls! Including you. Anyway, I just wanted to grab an eclair, if that's possible."

Meghan nodded and fetched an eclair from the kitchen. As she wrapped the sweet in the bakery's signature yellow paper, she wrinkled her forehead in confusion. Meghan was perturbed by the conversation Kayley and Tim had shared; Tim sounded *pleased* that Tom had been killed, and she felt goosebumps on her arms as she handed him his eclair.

"Thanks, Meghan. Good to see you. You have a truly sweet day," Tim joked as he walked toward the door.

Meghan turned to see Karen walk into the front of the bakery, her mouth agape. "Did you hear all of that?"

Karen nodded, her eyes large. "Yep. I heard every word. It sounds like we need to add another suspect to the list; Tim Dollar sounds *guilty,* and I think we might have our guy now."

10

Meghan nervously bit her fingernails as she walked up the pathway to Kayley's house. Kayley had called the previous night to confirm her request for a fruit cake to serve at her son's birthday party, and Meghan had agreed to fill the order. As she approached Kayley's beautiful home, she could feel her heart beating nervously in her chest.

"Meghan," Kayley greeted her as she flung open the door. "So glad you are here."

Meghan stepped into the entryway of Kayley's elegant home and gasped. "This is a lovely home, Kayley," she gushed.

Kayley snapped her gum dismissively. "It was all I got in my divorce," she shrugged. "It's fine. You brought the cake, yeah?"

Meghan nodded and held up the yellow cardboard box containing the cake. "It's my first fruitcake, but I think your son will like it!"

Kayley bit her lip. "I hope so," she whispered. "This party is already off to a strange start."

Meghan cocked her head to the side, yelping as she felt Siesta and Fiesta nipping at her ankles. "Oh! I hope it's okay that I brought my dogs. You mentioned that you have a dog, and I wanted my dogs to get some fresh air."

Kayley shrugged. "Whatever," she answered. "It's fine. Your dogs are the least of my worries today."

Meghan followed Kayley into the kitchen. She studied Kayley's outfit. Kayley was dressed in a tight red skirt and a matching jacket. She wore her signature high heels and matching lipstick. Meghan knew she could never pull off such a look, and she pulled nervously at her party dress, a navy blue tea-length frock with large white polka dots across the skirt.

"She came to the party," Kayley hissed as Meghan tugged at her skirt. "*She* came. It's so uncomfortable, Meghan; I extended an invitation to her before the scandal at the movie theater, and she still had the audacity to show up. Granted, I only invited her so I could find out if her husband would think about selling the theater to me, but now, he's dead, and she's still here, and it's terribly classless."

Meghan raised an eyebrow. "Who is here, Kayley? Are you talking about Sheila?"

Kayley nodded. "Yes. Sheila Doncaster is here. I invited her in the first place so that I could pick her brain about her husband's business plans, but now that her husband is dead, there is no reason for her to be here!"

Meghan bit her lip. "But she doesn't have children. Why would you invite someone without a child to your son's party?"

Kayley rolled her eyes. "You are so naïve, Meghan. I needed to talk with her, and this was the perfect excuse to have her over."

Meghan sighed. "Whatever you say, Kayley."

Kayley glared at Meghan. "It's just a disaster, Meghan.

First, she shows up here, and she's dressed like trash. You should see her. She looks like trash. It's a child's birthday party, for goodness sake!"

Meghan peered out the kitchen window. The party was taking place in Kayley's immaculately decorated backyard, and Meghan could see Sheila holding court amidst the Sandy Bay mothers. While Sheila was approximately the same age as the Sandy Bay mothers, her age was the only similarity between her and the other women; her hair was long and flowing, and she was dressed in a designer dress and dripping in diamonds.

"She looks ridiculous," Kayley hissed. "She says that this is her official goodbye to Sandy Bay. Upon her arrival, she announced to the group that she is leaving for an extended-stay luxury cruise and that we won't be seeing her for a long time."

Meghan stared at Kayley. "She said that to you?"

Kayley nodded. "Good riddance, though. Sheila has always been spoiled and sassy, and drama just seems to follow her all over the place. She couldn't keep her eyes on her own husband and look what happened to him. Everyone in town knew about her interest in that fitness instructor, Trevor. I think Sandy Bay will be better off without Sheila, and after the gauche way she showed up here, I'm of half a mind to tell her that myself!"

Meghan's jaw dropped. "So she's leaving? Indefinitely?"

Kayley shook her head. "I just said that. Aren't you listening to me, Meghan Truman?"

Meghan said nothing. She reached into her red purse and retrieved her cell phone, walking out of the kitchen and leaving Kayley alone. Meghan hastily dialed Jack's phone number, praying that he would pick up. She felt relieved when she finally heard his voice after the third ring.

"What's up, Meghan? I thought you were delivering a cake to Kayley Kane's kiddie party?"

Meghan stepped outside the house and into the side-yard, hoping that no one would overhear her conversation. "Jack," she whispered. "Sheila Doncaster, Tom's wife? She's leaving town, Jack. She's leaving town indefinitely, and she just announced it to a group of women at the party."

Jack said nothing, and Meghan gripped the phone harder, her stomach tossing and turning as she grappled with Kayley's words. "Jack?"

Meghan heard Jack shifting in his chair. "Meghan," he said slowly. "Is anyone around you right now?"

Meghan looked left and looked right, seeing no one. "No," she responded. "Everyone is in the backyard for the party. I stepped outside into the side-yard."

"Good," he said with relief in his voice. "Good. Meghan, I need you to listen to me. We had some breaks in the case today, and I need you to do a huge favor for me."

Meghan's heart beat faster and faster. "What is it, Jack?"

"Meghan," he whispered. "Do not let Sheila Doncaster leave that house."

"What?" she asked.

"Do not let Sheila Doncaster leave that house," he repeated. "I need you to do everything you can to keep her there. It is imperative that I talk to her immediately, and I need you to make sure she doesn't run!"

Jack hardly ever asked for any favors from Meghan, but as she stepped back into Kayley's house, she was determined to do all she could to ensure Sheila was still present when Jack arrived. As she made her way to where Sheila was holding court, she spotted Kayley's son and his friends playing with Siesta and Fiesta. She bent down to give the dogs some treats which she had saved in her purse. The excited children all clamored to have the opportunity to feed the dogs. Meghan giggled as her dogs rewarded every child who gave them a treat with animated yelps. From the corner of her eye, she saw Sheila withdrawing from the group and making a phone call. It seemed if she didn't make a move then Sheila might make a quick getaway and wouldn't be there when Jack arrived. That was definitely not going to happen under her watch.

"Sheila Doncaster, you are under arrest!" Jack shouted as he marched into Kayley Kane's house.

"What is this?" Kayley shrieked as Jack snapped a pair of handcuffs around Sheila's thin wrists. "This is a children's birthday party, Detective Irvin! What do you think you are doing?"

Jack shook his head and adjusted the handcuffs around Sheila's hands. "Ms. Kane, please step back," Jack advised as Kayley began pawing at him. "I have reason to believe that Sheila is connected to the murder of Tom Doncaster, and I need to take her in immediately!"

The crowd gasped. "This is an outrage," Sheila said weakly as Jack ushered her into the house from the backyard. "I'm not connected to my husband's murder! This is a setup! All of you people are just jealous of me and want me locked away. I'm looking at you, Kayley Kane. And Meghan, I saw you staring at me in the gym. You are all just jealous, and it would make you all feel better about yourselves if I were gone."

No one responded to Sheila's accusations, and Jack

loaded her into the police car. "This is shameful," Kayley wailed as Jack's car sped away. "My son's party is ruined. Ruined!"

Later that evening, Jack called Meghan to update her on the situation at the police station. "I think we're making some strides with this, Meghan," he said as Meghan twirled a dark hair around her finger. "I got some interesting information today during my conversation with Sheila. You're never going to believe this…"

Meghan stared at the night sky through her bay windows. The stars were sparkling, and she sighed as Fiesta and Siesta growled at each other from beneath her bed. "What is it, Jack?"

Jack took a long breath. "I talked with Sheila and Trevor, that fitness instructor."

Meghan gasped. "Both of them? What did you find out?"

Jack paused. "It's strange, Meghan. They both have alibis, which we are verifying, but for now, we are keeping both of them in jail."

Meghan cocked her head to the side. "What were their alibis?"

Jack sighed. "I can't disclose that information yet, but I'm leery of both of those people; Sheila just seems sneaky, and Trevor has been nothing but nasty."

"I'm not surprised to hear that," Meghan admitted. "Trevor was so rude to me in that fitness class; he was nice at first, but when I made him angry… it became quite frosty in that gym studio."

"Yeah, I saw that awkward side today, but I didn't let that unnerve me," Jack explained. "Instead, I learned that they are both involved in a ring of illegal supplements being sold at the gym. Sheila has such fine taste, and Trevor couldn't give her the things she wanted, so they started selling supplements to gym members. It's totally illegal, and my guys are all over it."

Meghan's jaw dropped. "An illegal supplement ring? That *is* crazy! What's going to happen now?"

"Like I said, we'll keep them in jail until we can verify their alibis. I'm pretty certain one of them shot old Tom, so once we figure out who did it, we can work on getting to the bottom of the illegal supplement ring and shut it down."

Meghan thought for a moment. With Tom's murder and her busy schedule at the bakery, she had not gotten to spend a lot of time with Jack lately, and she knew they were long overdue for some fun. She remembered how excited she had been when he had proposed date night a few weeks earlier, and Meghan smiled as she announced an idea.

"Jack," she began. "Let's go to the movies. I know things have been wild lately, but what would be better than a night out to take our minds off of things? That new manager, Tim Dollar, seems to like me a lot, and maybe he'll even give us our tickets for free!"

Jack took a long, slow breath. "I don't know if that is a good idea," he argued. "Meghan, the last time we went to the movies, Mrs. Sheridan threw a fit, and someone was killed. It just seems like bad luck to go back to the place where tragedy struck on our last date. Can't we just go bowling instead? Or play mini-golf? Come on, what do you think? Mini-golf sounds like fun to me."

Meghan pursed her lips. She thought of herself and Jack curled up together in the dark movie theater, his strong arms around her shoulders as they watched a romantic comedy together. Meghan's stomach fluttered as she imagined Jack leaning over during the movie to share a little kiss, and she knew that she had to hold her ground.

"I don't want to mini-golf, Jack," she said firmly. "I want

my handsome, sweet boyfriend to pick me up and take me to the movies."

Jack laughed. "Okay, beautiful," he relented. "I'll pick you up for the evening horror movie. How does that sound?"

Meghan shook her head. "Jack," she said. "No, no, no. The last time we went to the evening horror movie, someone was murdered. Tonight, we're seeing the romantic comedy!"

Jack chuckled. "That sounds like fun, Meghan," he agreed. "I could really use a story with a happy ending after all we've had going on over the last few weeks."

"For sure," Meghan affirmed. "And who knows, Jack; maybe it isn't too late for a happy ending after all."

Sinking into the soft, leather seat in the movie theater, Meghan folded her arms across her chest. Her visions of a sweet, romantic night out at the movies had been crushed only moments into the film; Jack was snoring heavily beside her, and she realized that the film featured an actress she detested.

"This is a joke," she muttered angrily to herself as she glared at Jack sleeping beside her. She had woken him up the first time he had fallen asleep, but after he told her that sleeping in the movie theater was "the best sleep he had ever had", she decided to leave him alone.

"So much for my romantic date night," Meghan grumbled as Mrs. Sheridan shrieked and moaned. Despite avoiding the concession stand this time, Meghan and Jack had run right into Mrs. Sheridan as they purchased their tickets. They were dismayed to find that she was seeing the same film as them, and Meghan grew more and more frustrated with every loud wail Mrs. Sheridan made.

"No! Don't kiss her! She's bad! She's an awful lady!" Mrs.

Sheridan screeched as the male lead leaned in to kiss the female lead in the film.

Meghan balled her hands into fists and shook her head. She was annoyed, but she tried to maintain her composure. "I'm going to the restroom," she whispered to Jack as she rose to venture to the ladies' room. Jack did not stir, and Meghan wandered down the dark hallway into the bright lights of the theater's corridor.

Meghan walked past three theaters, shaking her head. She was startled to run into an elderly woman in a wheelchair.

"Excuse me," the elderly woman whispered. "My chair is stuck, and I can't remove the brake. Can you help me?"

She bent down to help fix the brake. "Goodness, it's pretty stuck there." Meghan worked the lever of the brake back and forth. "I can't get it. Let me see if I can go find someone who can help."

The elderly woman nodded gratefully, and Meghan walked to an office. "Hello?" Meghan called as she gently opened the door. "Mr. Dollar? Are you in here? Is there a manager around?"

Meghan stepped inside the office and gasped. Tim Dollar was sitting in a chair, tears streaming down his face and his mouth agape. "Mr. Dollar?" Meghan shrieked. "What is going on?"

Meghan looked to the right and saw Ryan Branson in the corner. He was glaring at Tim Dollar and pointing a gun at Tim's shaking body.

"Ryan?" Meghan cried. "Ryan? What are you doing?"

Ryan bared his teeth as Meghan began to quake. "Meghan, I'm sorry you got wrapped up in this, but I'm going to need you to quietly close the door and have a seat."

Meghan obeyed. She silently pulled the door shut and sat in the empty chair next to Tim. "What is going on here, Ryan?"

Ryan closed his eyes and sighed. "I didn't want it to come to this, Meghan," he murmured. "This isn't what I wanted. But it's what has to happen."

"Please," Tim Dollar pleaded as Ryan lifted the gun to Tim's head. "Please don't do this!"

Meghan waved her hands in front of Ryan's face. "Ryan, tell me what is happening? Why are you doing this?"

Ryan growled. "He canceled my contract," he explained gruffly to Meghan. "This new fancy manager from New York canceled the contract between my confectionary and the movie theater. I'm losing a huge chunk of business, Meghan. I can't let that stand."

Meghan turned to look at Tim. "Mr. Dollar, can't you just restore the contract and let this go? Please?"

Tim shook his head. "It was not entirely my decision," he told Meghan in a shaking voice. "Headquarters did not like the contract and advised me to do away with it. I didn't want the deal, and headquarters gave me permission to let it go."

Ryan grimaced. "This is going to kill my business, so instead, I am going to kill *him*."

Meghan bit her lip. "That's crazy, Ryan. That is unlike you. You are a treasured member of this community, and you have been for years. You are not a killer, Ryan. You are a business owner and a staple of Sandy Bay. You aren't a cold-blooded killer."

Ryan turned to stare into Meghan's eyes. "But I am, Meghan," he whispered.

Meghan raised her eyebrows. "What did you say?"

Ryan sighed. He looked down at the floor, and then looked back at Meghan, hanging his head. "I *am* a cold-blooded killer, Meghan. I did away with that old manager, and I'll do away with the new one."

Meghan gasped. "*You* killed Tom Doncaster? Ryan, you

didn't. I've known you and respected you since I arrived in town all of those months ago. Please tell me you are lying."

Ryan shook his head. "I wish it were different, Meghan. I'm embarrassed that it's come to this. Things just got so crazy with my finances, and Tom was threatening to end my contact a few weeks ago, and I had to end *him*. I hoped that the new manager would keep the contract, but now, this fellow is telling me that headquarters wants him to end it."

Tears poured from Tim's eyes. "I'll talk to corporate," he pleaded. "I'll beg them! I'll tell them that your contract will stand. I'll do anything. Anything. Please?"

Ryan gripped the gun tighter. Meghan could see his hands were shaking, and she gently rose from the chair and edged toward him. "Ryan," she said quietly. "Put the gun down. Put it down, and we will all walk out of here like nothing happened. Right, Tim?"

Tim nodded. "That's right. I'll call headquarters in New York, and I'll personally make the arrangements to have your contract with this movie theater reinstated. I'll even request contracts with other local theaters to boost your business. We can all win here."

Ryan gritted his teeth and ran a hand through his curly hair. "Lies! You're lying! It's just too late for all of that," he said. Meghan could see the tears in his eyes, and she continued walking toward him.

"Stop, Meghan," Ryan ordered. "Back up. I'm sorry I have to do this, but it's too late. I'll make it quick, I promise…"

Meghan sat down in the chair and began to scream. "Stop that," Ryan ordered. "Stop screaming!"

Meghan continued to howl, and suddenly, there was a loud crash and a burning smell. Meghan looked at the wall above her and saw a small, gaping hole.

"Look what you made me do," Ryan cried. "Now, I have to

shoot the both of you. Sit down and shut up. It will all be over soon."

Ryan shuffled over to Meghan and held the gun against her skin. She shivered as the cool, hard metal touched her forehead, and she gagged as Ryan began to pull the trigger.

"I'm sorry, Meghan," he whispered.

"Please don't do this," Meghan shuddered as Ryan's finger moved. She closed her eyes as his finger continued to shift the trigger. Meghan gasped as she heard a small click. Ryan had pulled the trigger, and there was no going back.

"Stop right there!"

The trio turned to see Jack burst through the doors of the office. His own gun was drawn, and he pointed it at Ryan's head. Meghan opened her eyes. Ryan had dropped the gun on the floor, and Meghan dove for it, picking it up and examining it as Jack apprehended Ryan.

"It misfired," Meghan said in amazement as she looked at the gun that had failed to kill her. "I'm alive."

"You are under arrest, Ryan Branson," Jack stated as Tim fainted. "Mrs. Sheridan's wailing woke me up from the movie, and I realized Meghan was gone. When I came to find her, I stumbled upon the elderly woman in the wheelchair. She had heard everything, Ryan, and she told me where to find Meghan. Thank goodness I arrived in the nick of time."

Ryan collapsed onto the floor as Jack fastened the hand-cuffs around his wrists. "This isn't like me, Detective Irvin," Ryan moaned as Jack surveyed his handiwork. "This is not like me. My finances were messed up, and I acted too fast when I killed Tom. I didn't want to do it. I just broke down."

Jack glared at Ryan. "Save your sob story for the station,"

he spat at Ryan. "You tried to kill my girlfriend. I don't want to hear any more of your sob story before I have to."

Ryan began to weep as Jack led him outside. Meghan's hands shook as she carried the gun outside. "That was a close call," she said to herself. "If that gun hadn't misfired…"

"It was the gingerbread curse!" Mrs. Sheridan declared, scaring Meghan.

"I didn't see you there, Mrs. Sheridan," she said, her heart pounding.

"I heard the commotion and came out of the theater," Mrs. Sheridan explained. "It sounds like the gingerbread curse has happened again."

Meghan shook her head. "No," she said firmly. "The gun misfired and I wasn't killed. If that isn't good luck, I don't know what is. The curse is broken, Mrs. Sheridan, and I want you to know that, once and for all."

One week later, life had returned to normal in Sandy Bay. After the bullet retrieved from Tom Doncaster's body had been matched to the gun that had nearly killed Meghan, Ryan had been charged with murder. Sheila and Trevor had been released from jail with a hefty fine and were instructed to cease their illegal activities. Meghan even made a special batch of gingerbread cookies to celebrate the capture of the murderer, and admittedly, to spite Mrs. Sheridan a bit.

"Trudy?" Meghan called out to her assistant as she wiped her hands on her apron. "Trudy, we are closing the bakery for the day."

Trudy bustled out of the kitchen, still tanned from her week of vacation. "Oh?"

Meghan nodded. "There's been so much stress around this town lately, and with all the activity from the murder and the investigation, I need a break."

Trudy smiled. "That's good, Meghan. You need that."

Meghan grinned. "So do you, Trudy. Let's take the day off and start afresh tomorrow."

Trudy bid Meghan farewell, and Meghan called Jack. "I closed the shop for the day," she informed her boyfriend as she smiled. "I have an idea…"

Jack sighed. "Please tell me this doesn't involve going to the movies."

"It does," Meghan replied gleefully. "Third time is a charm, right? Let's go, Jack! The gingerbread curse is over, and the day is young. Let's have our little movie date and do it right this time. I'll even buy you a coffee beforehand so that you can enjoy the entire film. What do you say?"

"I say that I would do anything to spend time with you," he gushed as Meghan blushed. "When I saw Ryan pointing the gun at you last week, I thought I was going to lose you. It made me think about us and our relationship, and I just want to do everything in my power to make you the happiest girl in the world, Meghan Truman. If that means drinking a coffee or two and seeing a romantic comedy, you can count me in."

Meghan beamed. "Perfect. We'll have a wonderful date night. I'm looking forward to it, Jack."

When Jack and Meghan arrived at the movie theater, they did not stop at the concession stand; their pockets were stuffed with warm, fresh gingerbread cookies that Meghan had baked that morning. "It will be our little sweet treat," she whispered mischievously to Jack as he laughed.

They were both pleased to see that Mrs. Sheridan was not at the movies, and they settled into their seats for the third time in nearly a month. "I hope we get a happy ending this time," Jack whispered to Meghan as the previews began playing.

Meghan looked over into Jack's blue eyes. She felt her body grow warm and she reached over and took his hand.

Jack leaned over the armrest of his chair and took Meghan's face in his hands. He bent down to kiss her on the forehead, and slowly, he kissed her tenderly on the lips.

Meghan closed her eyes, thinking of her time in Sandy Bay, and how happy she was to have settled into her new life as a business owner, a dog mother, and now, as a girlfriend. "I think we'll get a happy ending this time, Jack," Meghan declared as the credits began to roll. "I think we'll get the happiest ending of all."

The End

HOT CHOCOLATE AND COLD BODIES

ABOUT HOT CHOCOLATE AND COLD BODIES

Released: November, 2018
Series: Book 8 – Sandy Bay Cozy Mystery Series
Standalone: Yes
Cliff-hanger: No

The end of year Sandy Bay festival is an opportunity for the town to display its history, promote local businesses and attract visitors to the best kept secret in the Pacific Northwest. There's just one problem. It's always associated with an increase in crime. This year, a stranger with an unknown identity is found dead during the fireworks display.

Some of the town's residents have had enough of the annual hassle. Others would rather die than see an end to this popular festival. Meghan Truman, a new resident in Sandy Bay with a successful bakery, is torn between either supporting an event that shines a light on all the good things about her adopted hometown or showing allegiance to a dear friend who is leading the cause to ban the festival.

With the town on the brink of a riot, no forthcoming clues to help Detective Jack Irvin in his murder investigation, Meghan must retain the hot passion that has seen her business and relationships prosper thus far while she confronts cold bodies all around.

The clock is ticking...

A murder investigation is growing cold...

Will Meghan provide the spark that unlocks this murder mystery?

1

I t was a crisp, fall day in Sandy Bay, and as Meghan Truman descended the stairs of Truly Sweet, her beloved bakery, she could sense that something was about to happen. She could not quite put her finger on it; while Sandy Bay was a small town in the Pacific Northwest, Meghan had been through a lot during her short stint as a resident, and as the chilly air hit her face, she knew in her heart that she was on the precipice of another adventure.

"Fiesta, Siesta, come on, babies," she urged her little twin dogs as they slowly waddled down the steps. "Come, keep me company in the bakery! The fall festival is this week, and with the town being so busy with the setup, I think business will be a little slower than usual…"

As Meghan spoke, she heard a knock at the front door of the bakery. She glanced down at the watch on her left wrist; it was not yet nine in the morning, and the bakery was not open yet. Who could be at her door so early?

"Maybe it's Jack," Meghan wished as she smoothed down her wild, long dark hair. "He dropped off some bagels in the morning for me as a surprise last week. Maybe he brought more?"

Meghan's heart fluttered as she thought of her adoring, handsome boyfriend, Jack Irvin. Jack was a detective in Sandy Bay, and Meghan had been dating him for a few months. Meghan could hardly keep the smile off of her face when Jack was around; he was tall, with striking blue eyes and blonde hair, and Meghan was smitten with him.

"Oh," Meghan said to herself as she peered outside.

Jacqueline Peters, the owner of the new salon and beauty shop in Sandy Bay, stood outside of the bakery. Meghan could see Jacqueline frowning, and she groaned as she unlocked the door.

"I want to be hospitable," Meghan whispered to her two dogs who were nipping playfully at her ankles. "But I haven't had my coffee yet, and I was hoping it would be Jack at the door…"

As Meghan unlocked the yellow front door of the bakery, Jacqueline came sweeping in.

"Meghan," she said kindly. "So good to see you this morning."

Meghan raised an eyebrow. "Good to see you too, Jacqueline," she replied slowly. "Truly Sweet isn't open for business yet, though."

Jacqueline shook her head. "I'm not here for treats today, Meghan," she informed Meghan. "I'm here in a professional capacity."

Meghan cocked her head to the side in confusion. "What do you mean?"

Jacqueline took a deep breath. "I know we are in different fields," she began. "You sell treats, and I make people beautiful."

Meghan nodded. "I know," she agreed. "You do. Every time I have had something done at your salon, I've loved the result; your stylist, Amelia, did a beautiful balayage on my hair two weeks ago, and I've gotten so many compliments!"

Jacqueline beamed. "Well, I'm thrilled you've been pleased," she said. "But I'm here today to ask you some questions as two businesswomen in a small town. Meghan, you are a small business owner. How did Truly Sweet fare when it first opened?"

Meghan bit her bottom lip and thought back on her first few days in town. The bakery had seen its ups and downs, but ultimately, Meghan was proud that she had persevered and grown her business to its current state of success. After a few setbacks and many, many triumphs, Truly Sweet was now one of the most popular bakeries in the area, and Meghan knew that her hard work had paid off.

Meghan opened her mouth to explain this to Jacqueline, but Jacqueline immediately cut her off.

"Let me explain, Meghan," she began. "My business has been growing so slowly! I'm getting frustrated, and part of me wants to throw in the towel. I knew I could come to you for some insight; you are a relatively new business owner, and you always seem so sweet."

Meghan smiled at the compliment. "That's kind of you to say," she told Jacqueline. "I understand that business can be slow in the beginning, but you can't give up. Your salon is fantastic; my hair has never looked or felt better, and the service I received was top notch. Don't give up on yourself yet, Jacqueline. There are so many possibilities that happen when you believe in yourself. Just give it a chance."

"Good morning, ladies!"

Meghan and Jacqueline looked to the front door where Kirsty Fisher, one of Sandy Bay's most dedicated citizens, marched through the front door. "You're open early today, Meghan? I was popping by the stationary store to pick up new business cards, and I saw that you were in."

Meghan shook her head. "I had a surprise visitor. Kirsty, do you know Jacqueline?"

Kirsty nodded at Jacqueline. "You own that salon just across the way? I've had my nails done there before; what a darling place. My cuticles have never looked nicer!"

Jacqueline blushed. "That is so nice of you to say."

Kirsty shrugged and adjusted the string of pearls around her neck. "I like to maintain my image, and it is not always easy to do that here in a small town. When your salon opened, I was delighted to find a place that meets my standards."

Meghan grinned. "See, Jacqueline? Business might be slow right now, but in this room, you have two happy customers."

Kirsty wrinkled her nose. "Business is slow?" Kirsty asked Jacqueline. "Well, I have a solution for you. I was going to come by later to invite you, Meghan, but it sounds like I will be inviting both of you! Ladies, at the Sandy Bay Fall Festival, Sandy Bay's most beloved annual event, we try to celebrate Sandy Bay's culture and local businesses. Would you two be interested in serving hot chocolate at one of our booths? You can decorate it with items from your stores, and you can pass out business cards."

Jacqueline looked to Meghan nervously. "What do you think?"

Kirsty interjected. "Meghan, you don't even have to bring treats! Both of you could simply show up, serve hot chocolate, and gain some valuable exposure for your businesses. What do you say?"

Meghan pondered the idea for a moment. Her business was booming, but she knew Jacqueline needed some help and encouragement. Meghan did love hot chocolate, and serving the toasty drink on a chilly evening at the fall festival sounded like the perfect seasonal activity that would warm

Meghan's heart, promote the bakery, and help Jacqueline Peters.

"We'll do it," Meghan declared as Kirsty clapped her hands. "It will be a fun way to participate in the fall festival. What could possibly go wrong?"

2

"I've never seen so many people in Sandy Bay!" Meghan exclaimed to Jack as they sat together at the bakery. Meghan had closed early for the evening; it was the first night of the Sandy Bay Fall Festival, and Jack had swung by the shop to pick her up for a night of fun.

"People from all over the Pacific Northwest come for the Sandy Bay Fall Festival," Jack explained to Meghan as he nibbled on an eclair. "It's truly spectacular! I've been going every year since I was born. The best part is the event by the water. The Pacific Ocean Fireworks Show is the grandest thing this town has ever seen. I can't wait for you to see it. Everyone goes out by the beach for a fireworks show that puts anything else to shame."

Meghan beamed. "People have been in and out of the bakery all day. It's been such a boost for my business to have so many people hustling and bustling around town."

Meghan and Jack turned as someone knocked on the door. "We're closed!" Meghan called out as the knocking continued. Meghan walked to the door to find a young couple smiling at her.

"Can we grab a cup of coffee?"

Meghan smiled apologetically. "We just closed, actually."

"Oh," said the young woman. "Bummer!"

Meghan pointed down the street at the festival. "But there are treats and drinks down there for the festival."

The man smiled. "We know," he explained. "We flew in from Dallas just for the festival; we stumbled upon it a few years ago when we were driving through Sandy Bay, and it was amazing! We've come back every single year since."

Meghan beamed. "That's wonderful. Well, how about this, I am working at the hot chocolate stand later. If you two come say hi, I will give you some hot chocolate, but I'll also bring some espresso from my shop to add in for a little treat."

"That would be lovely," said the man. "We hope to see you there."

Meghan waved goodbye and turned to Jack. "They were so nice," she said. "I can't believe people come in from all over to come to our festival. How special."

Jack nodded solemnly. "Not only is the festival great for Sandy Bay families, but it is also great for Sandy Bay businesses. We are so fortunate to have such an affair in town."

Meghan reached across the table to squeeze Jack's arm. "I'm so glad we get to share it together, Jack."

Jack leaned over and kissed Meghan gently on the lips. Meghan's stomach fluttered at his touch, and she felt her face burning as Jack leaned back to grin at her. "I'm glad we got to share *that* too."

Meghan and Jack stared at each other like two teenagers in love until a loud interruption stole their attention.

"Meghan, my money has been stolen."

Meghan and Jack broke their gaze and turned toward the door. Jacqueline had burst through, a distraught look on her face. Meghan bit her lip. She was eager for the fun night out with her boyfriend; Meghan and Jack were both so busy that date nights did not occur as often as they would like, and now Jacqueline was keeping them from the fall festival.

"Be kind," Meghan told herself as she forced herself to smile. "Jacqueline is new to town and has had some slow days with her business. I must be gracious."

Jacqueline rushed over to the table where Meghan and Jack had been lounging, her eyes wide and her face pale. "It's gone, Meghan. The money is *gone.*"

"What money?" Jack asked, transforming instantly from Jack Irvin the boyfriend, into Jack Irvin, Sandy Bay Detective.

Jacqueline buried her face in her hands. "The petty cash from my salon. I usually leave it in an envelope tucked behind a picture on the wall, and when I went to get some of the money today, the entire envelope was gone. The picture was askew. Someone had to have been back there."

Jack pulled out a pen and a tiny notepad from his pocket. "Can you give me more information?"

Before Jacqueline could speak, Rachel Rose, the owner of the local pet grooming shop, burst into the bakery. "Officer Irvin, I need your help."

Jack raised an eyebrow. "Rachel, I'm sorry, but I'm off duty. I'm helping take some notes for Jacqueline here, and then I am through for the day. Can you go to the police station? I'm sure there'll be someone there to help."

Rachel shook her head. "I was just on my way there and then I saw you in the window," she explained, pointing at the front window of the bakery. "My store has been vandalized. There is spray paint all over the back. Someone painted obscene words onto my store."

Jack shook his head. "I'm sorry that happened," he said gently to Rachel. "The Sandy Bay Fall Festival is a wonderful thing for the town, but sometimes, it attracts the wrong crowd. I'm going to guess that both of these situations are connected to the festival; perhaps a hoodlum from another town wandered to both of your stores—they are close to each other, aren't they?"

Both women nodded, and Meghan felt her chest sink. "Jack, with that kind of trouble out there, should *we* go to the fall festival? What if someone vandalizes Truly Sweet while I am away?"

Jack frowned. "I thought about that earlier," he admitted. "Unfortunately, incidents of vandalism and theft in town always increase during the festival. You have to make a choice though, Meghan. Do you want to sacrifice all of your fun at the festival just to sit home and wait for something to happen, even if it may *not* happen?"

Meghan shook her head. "No, that does sound silly."

Jack bid a farewell to Jacqueline and Rachel, and then, seeing the distress on Meghan's face, he took her into his arms. "Hey," Jack whispered. "We have extra patrols out tonight. I'll have them drive by the bakery a couple of times. Is that okay?"

Meghan leaned into Jack's hug. She turned to look up at him, and her heart started beating furiously in her chest. Jack *always* took care of her, and Meghan had no doubt that he was right; she could not waste the experience of going to the festival with Jack to sit home alone. Meghan smiled at Jack and pointed to the door. "You are right, Jack," Meghan told her boyfriend as he ran a hand through his blonde hair. "I can't live in fear. Let's go to the festival. I'm sure nothing bad will happen."

3

Jack's description of the fall festival had not done it justice; Meghan was in awe of the intricate decorations and beautiful lights, and she could not believe that Sandy Bay had transformed into an autumn wonderland.

"This festival has been amazing," Meghan cooed to Jack as they strolled through the booths and exhibits. "I can't believe it's the last day."

"Look at the string lights," Meghan murmured as they passed beneath a canopy of lights. "It's so romantic, Jack."

Jack winked. "My grandparents got engaged beneath that canopy of lights nearly sixty years ago. This festival is just full of tradition."

"And look at the booths. They all look like little castles, Jack. It's so sweet."

"You look the sweetest as the queen of the hot chocolate castle, Meghan. It's adorable watching you enjoy yourself."

Jack and Meghan walked past a mural that had been painted just for the festival. "This is lovely, Jack," Megan said. "I just wish it could be the festival forever."

Jack nodded. "It goes by so quickly. I love having something to look forward to after Halloween, and the festival committee does a great job putting it all together."

Meghan squeezed Jack's hand and shivered. It was a bitterly cold night; the cool winds were rolling in off of the Pacific Ocean and tearing through the town, and Meghan wished she had worn another sweater beneath her winter coat.

"Are you cold?" Jack asked Meghan as she shook. "Here, come closer to me."

Meghan's heart warmed as Jack pulled her close and wrapped an arm around her. "I'll keep you warm, Meghan Truman," Jack murmured as he leaned in and gave Meghan a small kiss on the lips.

"Hey, you kids."

Meghan and Jack turned to see Sally Sheridan, an elderly resident of Sandy Bay. She was known for her grumpiness, and Meghan groaned as Mrs. Sheridan approached, waving her cane up and down as she hobbled over to Jack and Meghan.

"That's enough of that kissing in public," Mrs. Sheridan lectured. "This is a family event, and we don't need that here."

Meghan and Jack nodded solemnly, but as Mrs. Sheridan walked away, Jack snuck another kiss. "Don't tell Mrs. Sheridan," Jack whispered as Meghan giggled.

The couple wandered through the rows of exhibits, both marveling at the decorations and the trinkets for sale. "This place has never looked more magical," Meghan breathed as she glanced up at the string lights twinkling above her. "And it smells wonderful. Sandy Bay really knows how to put on a party."

"Yes, we do," Jack agreed. "Hey, Meghan? It's nearly eight; isn't it your turn to run the chocolate booth?"

Meghan nodded. "Thanks for the reminder, Jack. It's my last shift, and I'm almost late. I will see you later?"

Jack grinned, and Meghan gave him a sweet kiss on the cheek. "Surely Mrs. Sheridan can't object to *that*," Meghan joked as she waved goodbye to Jack and walked to the hot chocolate booth.

"There you are," Kirsty said as Meghan approached. "We've been waiting for you."

"I'm not late," Meghan protested as she looked at the town clock tower in the distance. "The clock says it isn't even time yet, Kirsty."

"The early bird gets the worm, Meghan," Kirsty responded daintily as she held up her chin. "Anyway, I wanted to let you know that because it's the last night of the festival, we will just be giving away these last batches of hot chocolate. We've made so much money this week, and I'm comfortable letting the town have this treat."

Meghan smiled. "Great idea, Kirsty."

Meghan stepped into the booth and donned her apron. "Kirsty? Where is Jacqueline? Isn't she on this last shift with me?"

Kirsty shrugged. "She was assigned to work tonight, but I don't see her anywhere...."

Meghan scanned the crowd in front of the booth. She pulled out her cell phone to see if Jacqueline had called, but all she had was a missed call from Trudy, her assistant. "I haven't heard from her..."

Kirsty bit her lip. "Do you think you can manage here by yourself?"

Meghan casually waved her hand. "No problem," she answered. "Kirsty, I can do it. If Jacqueline shows up, she can help, if not, I can hold the fort in her absence."

"Well, if it gets too crazy, give me a shout," Kirsty said as she walked to the door. "Thanks again, Meghan. Enjoy."

Meghan happily manned the hot chocolate booth, enjoying the look of surprise on everyone's face as Meghan informed them the hot chocolate was free. After a half hour in the booth, Meghan heard an announcement, and she turned to face the main stage of the festival, peering at the structure from the little window of the booth.

"Good evening, everyone. My name is Tom Rose, and I am the proud Mayor of Sandy Bay," called out a tall, handsome blonde man from the center of the stage.

"Mayor Rose," Meghan said as she paused her hot chocolate making. "I haven't had the chance to meet him, yet. I'm excited to hear him speak."

"It's been a true treat watching everyone enjoy their time during the festival this week. Kirsty Fisher, we know that this could not have happened without you. Everyone give Kirsty a round of applause."

As the audience clapped, a man stumbled into the crowd standing just in front of the main stage. People turned to each other in confusion as the man bumped into people. The crowd backed away, mothers pulling their children into their arms and people looking annoyed at the man who had fallen to the ground.

"What is going on?" Meghan wondered as she squinted out of the window.

"Sir?" Mayor Rose asked. "Sir? Are you alright? Can we get some security in here? We have a man who is running into people and stumbling about. I think he may have had too much hot chocolate tonight."

The crowd gave a good-natured chuckle, and Meghan saw Jack approach the stumbling man. Before Jack could reach him, the man collapsed, falling motionless to the ground.

"Security? Ahhh, Detective Irvin, can you help our friend,

here?" Mayor Rose said softly into the microphone as Jack bent down to check on the man.

Meghan saw the color drain from Jack's face as he touched the man's wrist. Jack placed a hand on the man's forehead and then reached for the walkie-talkie in his back pocket. He pulled it to his mouth and spoke into it, his face frantic. Meghan saw his mouth move, and she wondered what was going on.

"Detective Irvin?" Mayor Rose asked.

Jack rose to his feet. "He's dead," Jack informed the mayor as the crowd began to scream. "This man is dead, Mayor Rose."

4

As the autumn winds howled outside, Meghan snuggled in her warm bed with Fiesta and Siesta resting on her lap. She nervously plucked a stray thread from her plum-colored turtleneck, wishing she had not been present to see the man fall over dead at the festival. As Meghan recounted the evening, she felt tears brim in her eyes; Jack had jumped straight into the investigation of the man's death, and many people at the festival were interviewed, including Meghan. She had finally arrived home at nearly two in the morning, and after the intense questioning, Meghan was exhausted.

"I can't believe no one knew who he was," Meghan murmured to Fiesta as the dog licked her cheek.

The dead man was a stranger to Sandy Bay; no one knew who he was, or why he was in town. The police had already begun to flood the town's social media outlets with pictures of the man, asking for any information to help identify him, and Meghan could not ignore the deep sense of dread in her stomach each time the man's face flashed before her eyes as she browsed through her phone.

"If they show another picture of this man again on the internet, I am going to have nightmares," Meghan fretted as an alert flashed across her screen.

The next morning, as Meghan was cleaning tables in the dining area of the bakery, she heard the familiar chime of bells, alerting her that someone had entered her shop. She looked up to find Kayley Kane, a local real estate agent.

"Can't believe what happened at the festival," Kayley said as she examined the counter filled with fresh pastries. "It's like we can never get a quiet stretch in this town."

Meghan yawned. "I know, Kayley," she agreed. "When I decided to move here, I didn't expect a small town in the Pacific Northwest to have so much action."

Kayley snapped her gum. "Ever since you showed up, things have been wild," she told Meghan as she selected a peach scone. "Anyway, you're busy cleaning tables. I'll leave my money on the counter. Have a good one, Meghan. Hope it's a quiet day."

At the end of the workday, Meghan realized she was running low on eggs. "Trudy?" Meghan called to her assistant.

"Yes, Meghan?" Trudy replied.

"We're low on eggs. I need six dozen to start prepping the treats for the morning breakfast crowds. Do you mind running to the grocery?"

Trudy frowned. "I have a doctor's appointment, remember? I need to get out of here early today."

Meghan shrugged. "I'll go. It's fine. I will run out right now and will be back to send you off to your appointment in fifteen minutes or so."

"Thanks, Meghan," Trudy said gratefully. "I'll see you in a bit."

A few minutes later, Meghan arrived at the grocery and fetched the eggs, but just as she was leaving, she heard shouting in the aisle behind her. Kirsty Fisher was screaming, and Meghan left her cart at the checkout line to see what was the matter.

"You will *not* cancel future fall festivals," Kirsty declared as she glared at Mayor Rose. Meghan peered around the corner, her mouth agape.

"Kirsty," Mayor Rose said cautiously. "Someone *died* at the last festival! Public safety is of the utmost concern to me, and if canceling the festival will save lives here, then so be it."

"Do you not understand how much I give to this town?" Kirsty asked, pointing a finger at the mayor and then driving it into his chest. "I give and give and give, and my favorite event to put on is this festival. You can't take this away from me because some *stranger* happened to die at the event. It's preposterous."

Meghan's heart beat quickly in her chest as she watched the mayor's face darken. "Take your finger off of me," he ordered Kirsty as she narrowed her eyes. "Ms. Fisher, I happen to have an excellent attorney who will go to town with the news that Kirsty Fisher assaulted the mayor in public. I advise you to step back and get yourself together. I have not decided for sure if we will cancel future fall festivals, but if you have an issue with that, you may make an appointment at the courthouse like *everyone else* does."

Kirsty folded her arms across her chest. "I don't see what the point of canceling the festival would be," she continued. "One little misfortune should not ruin things for everyone, Mayor Rose."

The Mayor's jaw dropped. "Kirsty, listen to yourself. Someone *died* at the fall festival, and you are more concerned about throwing your event. I'm surprised at you."

Kirsty rolled her eyes. "Well, I'm surprised at *you.* For someone who begs Sandy Bay residents to participate in town events, and for someone who *begged* my ex-husband

and me for financial support during his reelection campaign, I am shocked that you are open to the idea of canceling *my* fall festival. But, if you want to bring your lawyer into this, then I can too. I'll be calling your office first thing in the morning, Mayor Rose, and don't think that I won't."

Meghan watched as Kirsty held her head high and stormed out of the grocery store. The other patrons were staring at the mayor, and Meghan could hear their whispers as she returned to her cart.

"That fall festival should be canceled. Someone died! Kirsty Fisher is so selfish."

"We can't cancel the festival. That festival is a town event, and it has been for over a hundred years."

"We have enough festivals in this town. Let's just get rid of this one."

"That man is dead, and all Kirsty can talk about is her event? That's shameful."

Meghan paid for her eggs and walked home, the tight, hot feeling of dread growing in the pit of her stomach. She felt anxious as she ventured back to the bakery, shuddering at every shadow and cringing at any unexpected noises. "Kayley was right," Meghan muttered to herself as she recounted the altercation between Kirsty and the Mayor. "It's like we can never get a quiet stretch in this town, that's for sure."

5

"I just wish *someone* would identify him," Jack complained to Meghan as they sipped on tea at the bakery. "How can no one know who he is?"

Meghan nodded, stirring her earl grey tea with a little silver spoon. "It's a shame," she said sadly. "Can you imagine if one of your loved ones had died and no one told you? He must have someone out there who loved him and needs to mourn him. It's just terrible."

"We've spoken to nearly everyone in town, too," Jack told Meghan. "Almost everyone in Sandy Bay was out and about that night, and no one seems to know anything."

Meghan thought back to the night of the man's death. She remembered her shift in the hot chocolate booth, and then she recalled Jacqueline's absence.

"Do you guys think it was a murder?" Meghan asked Jack, her body growing cold.

Jack paused. "We don't know yet," he admitted as Meghan's eyes widened. "But his death was so odd; no one noticed him before he stumbled into that crowd, and then, before we all knew it, he was dead."

Meghan pursed her lips. She didn't know if Jacqueline was connected to the man's death, but it did seem odd that she hadn't shown up to her shift. Meghan had even called Jacqueline the next day, and Jacqueline did not respond.

Jack glanced at his watch and nearly fell out of his chair. "Oh no," he murmured as he rose from the table. "It's past my lunch break, Meghan. I talked for too long. This case just has me feeling frustrated. I really hate that no one has come forward to provide information about this guy. Thanks for listening to me."

"Any time, Jack," Meghan replied sweetly as she also rose from the table. She leaned up to give Jack a little kiss on the cheek. "I'm glad you spent your lunch hour with me. It was good to see you."

"Of course," Jack said as he put an arm around Meghan. "Seeing you makes my day, Meghan."

Later that afternoon, Meghan paid a visit to Jacqueline's salon. She had been thinking about the man's death, and she wanted to see if Jacqueline had the answers the police were looking for.

"Hello?" Meghan called as she walked inside. She tugged on Fiesta and Siesta's leashes; she had brought the dogs along for company, but they were now hopelessly tangled around Meghan's legs.

"Meghan?" Jacqueline called out as she emerged from the back of the salon. "What are you doing here?"

Meghan smiled. "You didn't show up to the hot chocolate booth," she explained. "I was worried about you, and with that man dropping dead…"

"Oh my," Jacqueline said as she fanned her face dramatically. "When I heard that news, I was so happy I stayed away that night. With those rough crowds in town for the festival, I can't say I'm surprised something happened. I'm just terrified someone is going to break into my salon again!"

Meghan tied the dogs' leashes to a chair and let them play, settling into a salon chair and spinning around to face Jacqueline. "Can I ask why you stayed away that night? We were supposed to run the booth together, Jacqueline."

Jacqueline paused, and Meghan saw her face darken. "It's really none of your business," Jacqueline snipped at Meghan.

Meghan folded her arms across her chest. "I'm just curious, Jacqueline. A man turns up dead on the night you bail on our hot chocolate booth? It just seems strange."

Jacqueline glared at Meghan. "You want to know where I was? Fine! I'll tell you. I flew home to my parents in Memphis to ask them for some money. My business is not picking up, and I needed some assistance. I have my flight records if you want to see them, Meghan."

Meghan's heart sank as Jacqueline burst into tears. "I'm sorry I intruded," Meghan said softly, walking over to Jacqueline and placing a hand on her shoulder. "Forgive me. I didn't mean to be callous, Jacqueline."

Jacqueline blew her nose on her sleeve. "I just want to make something of myself, you know? I want to grow this business and make it something huge."

Meghan nodded. "I get it," she said, running a hand through her long, wavy hair. "Growing a business from the ground up is difficult, but know that you're doing good work here, Jacqueline. I told you that you gave me the best hair I've ever had. Just believe in yourself and your dream."

"Thanks," Jacqueline said, wiping her tears and smiling weakly at Meghan. "I'm sorry I snapped at you. I'm just a little embarrassed at having to borrow money, and I didn't know what to say."

"It's all good," Meghan replied, throwing her arms around Jacqueline. "Just keep working hard and believe in yourself. It will all get better, I promise."

As Meghan walked home later that night, her cell phone

rang. It was Jack, and Meghan's voice was giddy as she answered. "Hey, stranger!"

"Hey, Meghan."

Meghan heard the seriousness in Jack's voice, and she bit her bottom lip. "What's wrong, Jack?"

Jack sighed. "We finally received some information," he informed Meghan. "We had a caller contact us on the hotline. He claims he knew the man who died."

Meghan gasped. "Who was it? What did he say?"

"He mumbled. We could hardly hear him, and then he hung up," Jack explained. "This is our first real break in the case. Just keep a lookout for suspicious things, Meghan. I have a bad feeling about this case, and a real gut feeling that something bad is going to happen sooner than later."

6

Meghan's chest tightened as she gripped the cup of hot chocolate she had just made for herself. It was a quiet afternoon in the bakery, and Meghan had not seen a customer in nearly an hour. The town was so unsettled from the strange death of the man, and people were not milling about as they normally did in the afternoon.

As Meghan sipped her hot chocolate, she heard the bells chime on the front door. Jack strode into the bakery, and Meghan's heavy heart fluttered. Meghan's excitement faded when she saw Jack's countenance; his face was serious and his eyes were dark, and Meghan knew something must be wrong.

"Jack?" Meghan asked.

Jack scowled. "It's bad, Meghan. We got some reports today, and it turns out that the fingerprints of that guy match fingerprints taken at Jacqueline's salon when we investigated the burglary."

Meghan's dark eyes widened. "You're kidding me…"

Jack shook his head. "The man had a gunshot wound, so Chief Nunan has ordered this to expand into a murder investigation. We had a call from the police department in Enfield, a neighboring town to Sandy Bay. They saw the dead man's picture on our social media feeds and confirmed who he was. He had a juvenile record for several petty crimes when he was a teenager, but it seems those records were expunged once he turned eighteen. That was why we couldn't identify him on any of the national databases. The officer who called said he had personally arrested him when he was young and restless. It looks like he didn't outgrow the restless part. I don't know if I like the looks of it, and I'm not so sure it was a murder, but what Chief Nunan says goes. I'm off to check in at the station, but I had to come by and see you. This town is all shaken up, and I want to remind *you*, my sweetheart, to stay safe."

Meghan's heart warmed as Jack pulled her into his arms. "Thank you for checking on me, Jack," she said sweetly as he stroked her head. "You are truly sweet."

After Jack and Meghan said goodbye, Meghan fetched a broom and began to sweep the dining area. She put in headphones and listened to upbeat music, needing to cheer herself up after what had been such a strange week in Sandy Bay.

"Meghan?"

Meghan nearly jumped out of her skin when she felt a tap on her shoulder. She turned around to find Trudy smiling at her. "Trudy, I nearly died of fright!" Meghan exclaimed as she placed a hand on her racing heart. "My headphones were in and I didn't hear you walk out from the kitchen. What's up?"

Trudy gestured at the back of the dining area where an elderly woman sat alone. "I heard the silver bells chime a few minutes ago when she came in, and when I didn't hear your voice serving her, I thought I should come check on things."

Meghan laughed. "What would I do without you, Trudy? I didn't even hear her come in! I'm so glad you came up here."

Trudy grinned as she walked back to the kitchen. "It's fine, Meghan. No problem. I'm just happy to help."

Meghan walked over to the elderly woman's table. The woman looked ancient, with hundreds of wrinkles etched deep into her face, and faded blue eyes. Her hands shook as they rested on the table, and Meghan felt her heart sink with sadness as she studied the old woman sitting all by herself.

"I didn't hear you come in," Meghan said as she crouched down next to the table. "My apologies for making you wait. I'm Meghan Truman, the owner of Truly Sweet. What can I get for you today?"

The old woman hung her head. Meghan noticed a tear falling slowly down the woman's lined cheek, and she took the seat across from her. "May I sit?"

The old woman nodded. Meghan plastered a smile on her face as the old woman gestured at the seat in front of her where she had sat down. "You look like you could use a friend," Meghan murmured as she reached across the table and took the old woman's shaking hands. Meghan pushed her own dark hair out of her eyes and took a deep breath. "So what brought you in today? Would you like some tea?"

The old woman shook her head. "There's been some turmoil in my family that's left a big hole in my heart, and I just wanted a respite from the sadness. Your little bakery looked so cozy when I walked by, and I just had to come in."

Meghan smiled. "I try to make this a comfortable, inviting place for everyone," she told the woman. "I'm glad you found your way here, and I am sorry to hear about the issues in your family."

The old woman's lips turned upward into a weak smile. "Thank you, dear girl," she said, her voice shaking. "It hasn't been easy, but that's how life goes, I suppose."

95

Meghan hung her head. "The ups of life can be remarkable, but the downs can be truly terrible. I'm sorry if I'm being too forward, but can you tell me what's causing the unrest in your family?"

The old woman thought for a moment and then answered, "Someone I love has been getting into a lot of trouble and it seems his latest escapade has brought me to this part of town to pick up the pieces."

Meghan bit her bottom lip. "Again, I'm so terribly sorry. I have to say that the love of family endures through thick and thin."

The old woman's blue eyes filled with tears, but she retrieved a worn handkerchief from her sleeve and dabbed her damp cheeks. "Excuse me," she whispered to Meghan.

Meghan frowned. "Please don't apologize," she told the woman. "It's okay to cry."

The two women chatted for nearly an hour, exchanging pleasantries, and eventually, Meghan told the woman her story of moving from Los Angeles to Sandy Bay. Just as Meghan finished her tale, the old woman looked down at the shabby watch on her wrist and shrieked. "It's too late! I've stayed too long; I have an appointment, and I must go."

Meghan squeezed the woman's hands. "Wait! Before you go….are you from Sandy Bay? I've only lived here for a few months, and I surely don't know everyone, but I don't think I've ever seen you before…."

The old woman closed her eyes and shook her head. "I'm not from around here," she told Meghan. "Just… stopping through."

Meghan nodded, staring at the woman's dark blue eyes that seemed to reflect a lot of personal heartache. "I see. Well, can I help you get to your appointment? Where are you headed?"

The old woman looked Meghan in the eyes. "I'm going to the morgue," she informed Meghan with a grim face. "I have to go identify my son's body. He passed away at some local fall festival? You may have heard about it?"

7

"**I** didn't do anything! I don't understand why I am always blamed for *everything* in this town!"

Meghan cringed as she heard Jamie Winston, the owner of a gun shop and the bar in town, screaming in Jack's office. She nervously played with the brown paper bag in her hands; she had stopped by the Sandy Bay Police Station to drop off a surprise lunch for Jack, but before he could see her, Jamie had been led into Jack's small office.

"Just wait outside, Meghan," Jack whispered as Meghan nodded. "Chief Nunan said he was pretty upset when he was picked up, and I know he can be a wild card sometimes."

Meghan had been waiting for nearly an hour as Jamie shouted at Jack. "I didn't do *anything*," he argued as Meghan heard Jack mumble behind the closed door.

"The dead man had a gunshot wound, and one of the guns from *your* store was recently reported missing. We only brought you in to get some information, Jamie, but this strong reaction makes me feel like there might be more to the story here. Is there?"

Meghan heard Jamie grunt. "No," he answered gruffly. "I

am just sick and tired of getting blamed for some of the crazy things that happen in this town."

Meghan looked down at her watch. She needed to return to the bakery soon, and while she wanted to deliver the lunch to Jack, she could not wait around forever. She rose from her chair and knocked on Jack's door. Jack appeared, but he did not open the door all the way.

"It's a bad time, Meghan," he whispered as Meghan shoved the bag into his hands. "What is this?"

"I made lunch for you," she said with a wink. "Just a little surprise for this dreary morning!"

Jack's eyes shone, and he leaned down to give Meghan a kiss on the cheek. "You are such a darling," he murmured. "I'll call you later, beautiful; Jamie is going on and on, and I don't think I can visit with you now."

"It's fine," she assured Jack. "No problem! I'm going to get on back to the bakery."

Before Meghan could turn to leave, Jamie opened the door all the way. He marched past Jack and glared at Meghan. "Can you believe this, Meghan? I'm in the middle of trouble again! I am so sick of this. That stupid man stumbled into the festival and just *died*. I had nothing to do with it. Sure, as the police tell me, he had a gunshot wound, but it could have been old. He probably just had too much hot chocolate."

"That's my son you are talking about."

Meghan, Jack, and Jamie turned to see the old woman from the bakery hobble down the corridor. Her eyes were red, and Meghan ran to her, taking her hand and helping her into a chair.

"What are you doing here?" Meghan asked in concern as the woman caught her breath.

"I wanted to see the police officer who is in charge of this investigation," the woman explained to Meghan. "I didn't expect to hear my son being talked about so nastily. My heart is just broken."

Jamie scowled. "This is just nonsense," he complained as he narrowed his eyes at the woman. "Your son has gotten me into a lot of trouble, lady. I'm not very happy about being here. I'm losing customers by not being in my store. I'm leaving, Detective Irvin. If you need me, have someone issue a warrant; I'm not coming back here just to chat."

Meghan gasped as Jamie stormed out of the station. She kneeled beside the old woman and took her hands. "I am so sorry you had to hear that—"

"Lou," the old woman answered. "My name is Lou."

"Lou," Meghan said soothingly as she looked to Jack for assistance. "Lou, I'm not sure where your son's things are, but Detective Irvin here will go check. Isn't that right, Detective Irvin?"

Jack nodded. "Absolutely. Ma'am, I will be right back with your things."

Jack scurried off, and Meghan slid into the chair next to Lou's. "I'm sorry he was being so rude," she said softly.

Lou buried her face in her hands. "No one really liked my son," she admitted. "He was difficult at times, and he always struggled to make friends. It still hurts a mother's heart to hear those things, though. It's all been so difficult."

Meghan nodded. "I'm sure. I cannot even imagine what you are going through. Please know that if you need *anything* at all, my door is always open for you, Lou."

Suddenly, Meghan heard a shout down the hallway. "What is going on?" Meghan asked aloud as she squinted her eyes and saw Karen Denton, one of her dearest friends, standing outside of a closed door, a huge sign in her hands.

"Karen?" she called out.

"Meghan!" Karen replied, dropping the sign and jogging to where Meghan and Lou sat.

"What's going on? What was that sign?" Meghan asked.

Karen smiled. "Mayor Rose is threatening to ban the fall festival because of the fellow who died," she informed Meghan as Lou shuddered. "Oh, hello there," Karen said as she made eye contact with Lou. "Who are you?"

Lou cleared her throat. "I am the mother of the *fellow* who died," she declared. "And I am *leaving* this police station. This place is nothing but chaos. I will get my son's things another time. Meghan, thank you for visiting with me. You are truly sweet."

Meghan and Karen stared as Lou slowly walked out of the police station. "That old lady was the mother of the dead man?" Karen asked.

Meghan nodded. "She's not much older than you, Karen," Meghan said as she stared at Karen's impressive athletic figure. "I imagine she's in her seventies or eighties."

Karen laughed. "I might be in my seventies, but my mind and my body are in my twenties, just like you. Anyway, that's so sad that she's here. But, life marches on, and so do I! So, Meghan? Do you want to join the movement? We are supporting the Mayor's festival ban, and we could always use more participants. That silly old festival brings nothing but shady crowds, pollution, and chaos to this town. Sandy Bay *needs* us to take a stand, and with Mayor Rose on our side, we can put an end to the festival once and for all! What do you say, Meghan? Are you with us, or against us?"

8

As Meghan iced a carrot cake later that evening at the bakery, she felt a knot in her stomach as she thought about her earlier interaction with Karen. Karen had pestered Meghan for nearly forty-five minutes to join the protest, but despite her friend's passion, Meghan was not convinced that a protest was the best idea.

"What if things go awry, Karen?" she asked, her dark eyes filled with concern. "What if things get out of hand?"

Karen scowled. "A protest in front of Mayor Rose's office is just what this town needs, Meghan! Sandy Bay *needs* to ban the fall festival."

"But someone *died* there, Karen," she countered in a hush tone. "I just don't think now is the time to fight this battle. Maybe voicing your own concerns with the festival at another time would be more appropriate?"

Karen rolled her eyes at Meghan and stormed off, leaving Meghan with hurt feelings. The two friends had never quarreled before; they had been friends for several years, and Karen was the person who had convinced Meghan to move to Sandy Bay in the first place. Meghan was devastated that

Karen had been so rude, and she had walked home with tears in her dark eyes.

"Meghan?"

Meghan looked up to see Mrs. Sheridan enter the bakery. Meghan stifled a groan; Mrs. Sheridan could be so difficult to deal with, and after her encounters with Jamie and Karen, Meghan was simply exhausted. Still, she put a smile on her face and greeted her customer.

"Hello, Mrs. Sheridan. It's a pleasure to see you today."

Mrs. Sheridan walked right up to Meghan and stared into her dark eyes. "We need to talk," Mrs. Sheridan declared in her raspy voice. "We need to talk about the protest. Karen Denton told me you don't think protesting the ban on the fall festival is a good idea?"

Meghan's jaw dropped. "I... didn't say that," she sputtered.

"Then what did you say?" Mrs. Sheridan asked as she tapped her cane impatiently on the wooden floor.

Meghan shook her head. "I'm not from Sandy Bay originally, Mrs. Sheridan," she told the old woman. "I shouldn't really have a say in this."

Mrs. Sheridan frowned. "You have lived here for several months, and you own a business here. You have a say, just like the rest of us."

Meghan's heart softened at Mrs. Sheridan's statement. Meghan had never felt accepted by Mrs. Sheridan, and to hear her say that Meghan deserved a say in the fall festival decision made Meghan feel included.

"Let me tell you a little story, Meghan. May we sit?" Mrs. Sheridan asked as she pointed her cane in the direction of the little white tables in the dining area.

Meghan nodded. "Of course, Mrs. Sheridan."

The two women walked to a table next to the window, and Meghan held out Mrs. Sheridan's chair. She seated herself once Mrs. Sheridan was settled. Meghan and Mrs. Sheridan sat across from each other, and Mrs. Sheridan began to speak. "This protest is *important*, Meghan," she informed Meghan.

"I know. Everyone in Sandy Bay loves the festival," Meghan agreed.

Mrs. Sheridan shook her head. "You don't understand," she said. "This isn't just about loving the festival, Meghan."

Meghan cocked her head to the side. "I'm confused," she said. "What is it about?"

Mrs. Sheridan sighed, clearing her throat and looking Meghan in the eyes. "The festival is part of our history and heritage here, Meghan. Sandy Bay's very existence is owed to that festival! Back in the 19th century, before the town was even established, pioneers met on this very ground to break bread and enjoy each other's company before the weather turned. The gathering became a treasured annual event, and eventually, some of those pioneers decided to stay in the area. The town was then established, and it's all only grown from there."

Meghan was fascinated. "I had no idea that is how this town was founded. How amazing!"

Mrs. Sheridan narrowed her eyes at Meghan. "That isn't the end of the story, Meghan. You *have* to understand why this festival is so important. For so many of us, it's where our own stories here in Sandy Bay began."

Meghan wrinkled her nose. "What do you mean?"

Mrs. Sheridan's eyes filled with tears. "Before the movie theater, and before the restaurants, all this town had was that festival. People met and fell in love at the fall festival. My own parents met there, many years ago. My father asked my mother to marry him at that festival. I told my late husband I was pregnant with our firstborn at the festival. It's the last place I went with my late husband before he became sick and passed away. That festival is part of this town, and without it, Sandy Bay loses its memories, its traditions, and its true heart and soul, Meghan."

Meghan tried to stifle her tears, but she could not hold back; her cheeks grew damp as she cried, and Mrs. Sheridan reached a hand across the table to wipe away a tear from Meghan's face.

"I know, it's quite the story, isn't it? This festival is just rich with history, and I cannot stand to see it vanish."

Meghan wiped her eyes. "Why are you telling me all of this?"

"I know I've been grumpy toward you before," Mrs. Sheridan admitted with a guilty look on her face. "I'm sorry. Ever since my husband died and my children moved across the country, it's been difficult for me to make new friends. I've also felt a little bitter toward you... you don't know this, but this location? These very grounds where your bakery sits? This is where generations of my own family used to own a general store. My grandparents' parents and their parents owned this very plot of land! We lost it during the great depression, when I was just a baby, and my parents never recovered from the heartbreak.

"Oh my goodness," Meghan whispered.

Mrs. Sheridan nodded. "I just have always had hate in my heart toward whoever owned this land... it isn't your fault, though. And now, Meghan, I want to let bygones be bygones. I need you though, Meghan. I *need* you. You are a business owner in this town; you have some influence. Please, Meghan. I'm begging you. Stand with us protesters as we demand the Mayor hear our voices. Stand on the right side of history. Stand with Sandy Bay."

9

"WE KNOW BEST! END THE FEST!"

"END THE FEST, WE WON'T REST!"

Meghan carefully navigated the enormous crowd gathered outside of the Sandy Bay Courthouse. The two groups were boisterous, each side equipped with a diverse array of signs and noisemakers.

"Excuse me," Meghan murmured as she stepped through the crowd. "Pardon me."

"Which side you on, kid?" Jamie Winston yelled at Meghan as she nearly dropped her own sign.

Meghan did not answer; she merely put her head down and walked silently to the group positioned right in front of the Mayor's window.

"You're here!" Mrs. Sheridan said gleefully as Meghan walked up to her. "So happy you are on our side, Meghan."

"I hate to choose sides," she admitted. "I can see the point in ending the festival due to that man's death. But, your story was so compelling, Mrs. Sheridan. I think the festival is part of this town's legacy, and I would hate to see that end."

Meghan felt a tap on her shoulder. Karen stood behind her with a frustrated look on her face.

"Meghan? What are you doing here? I thought you didn't think it was *appropriate* timing for any sort of fuss about the festival!"

Meghan sheepishly looked at Mrs. Sheridan and shrugged. "Karen," Meghan said gently. "Mrs. Sheridan and I had a nice visit the other day, and after thinking long and hard, I think the right thing for me to do is to support her and to support the fall festival."

Karen's jaw dropped. "Are you kidding me? That is a mistake, Meghan. This festival needs to go."

Mrs. Sheridan pushed her way in front of Meghan and drew herself up to full height, staring into Karen's blue eyes and shaking her head. "Look, youngun," Mrs. Sheridan said.

"Youngun?" Karen responded sassily. "Sally Sheridan, I'm not much younger than *you.*"

Mrs. Sheridan stuck out her tongue at Karen. "Karen Denton, you silly little girl. Why don't you go back to your little dance class and leave the protesting for us women?"

Karen's eyes widened, and Meghan had to stifle a laugh at the two older women facing off in the middle of the protest. "It's called *barre* class, Sally," Karen haughtily informed Mrs. Sheridan. "It's a wonderful way to build muscle and tone the legs! Maybe you should try it sometime instead of whining to Meghan here about your problems."

Mrs. Sheridan lifted up her skirt to her knees to reveal her thin, boney legs. "My legs are already real pretty, Karen," she said. "But yours won't be if you don't get out of my face!"

Meghan gasped as Mrs. Sheridan lifted her cane up. "I'll swing at those legs of yours, Karen, if you don't leave us alone. Go. Get on, now."

Karen turned on her heel and sprinted away from Meghan and Mrs. Sheridan.

"Mrs. Sheridan!" Meghan exclaimed. "You were going to hit Karen's legs? She is a devoted athlete! She would have been devastated."

Mrs. Sheridan turned to Meghan and winked. "I would never do that to old Karen Denton," she said slyly. "But it didn't hurt to scare her a little…"

Mrs. Sheridan hugged Meghan, but as they embraced, a man shoved past the two women and nearly sent Meghan to the ground.

"Hey!" Mrs. Sheridan yelled. "Get back to your side. We are supporters of the festival. You almost knocked my friend down. Get out of here!"

The man sneered at Mrs. Sheridan, but he returned to his side. "Those scoundrels," Mrs. Sheridan muttered. "This protest is getting out of hand. I'm surprised your fellow is not here to keep things under control."

Meghan laughed. "He's here," she giggled. "He's under-cover. He told me that I won't recognize him in his disguise, so I don't expect to run into him today."

As Meghan and Mrs. Sheridan chuckled, both crowds began to yell. "What's happening?" Mrs. Sheridan asked as Meghan pointed upward.

"Look!" Meghan shouted. "The Mayor is coming out onto his balcony. Everyone! Hold up your signs so he can see you; Mayor Rose needs to hear our voices and know our cause!"

Meghan's eyes widened as Mayor Rose stepped onto the small balcony two stories above the crowds. He gazed left and then gazed right.

"What do you think he's going to say?" Meghan asked Mrs. Sheridan, who shrugged.

"Attention, Sandy Bay residents," the Mayor began. "Pro-testors, I want to thank you all for being active citizens and getting involved in this…situation."

Mrs. Sheridan rolled her eyes. "This is not a *situation*," she scoffed. "This is a *shame* that he is threatening to take away our festival!"

The Mayor continued. "I care about this town, and clearly you do as well; from the count of the police officers stationed in the crowd, we have over four-hundred residents of Sandy Bay protesting today."

Meghan scanned the crowd for any sign of Jack, but she did not see her boyfriend. The Mayor cleared his throat and spoke even louder. "We have scheduled an emergency town hall meeting to discuss these issues. All are welcome. This is not the appropriate venue for me to make decisions or share information. The town hall meeting will be tomorrow evening. I invite you all to come. Thank you for being here."

As the mayor turned to step back inside the courthouse, Meghan saw Mrs. Sheridan slip her hand into her pocket. Meghan gasped. Mrs. Sheridan was holding a round, rotten tomato.

"This one is for my parents!" Mrs. Sheridan screeched as she hurled the tomato at the mayor. The tomato hit him square in the face, and the crowd broke out in screams.

"The Mayor has been shot! Look at his bloody face!"

"Attack! Attack on the Mayor!"

People ran wild as Mrs. Sheridan pulled out a moldy potato from her purse. "This one is for my late husband!" Mrs. Sheridan lifted her arm to hurl the potato at the mayor who was awestruck on the balcony, but before she could throw it, she was apprehended by Jack Irvin.

"What are you doing, Mrs. Sheridan?"

Jack snatched the potato and put it in his own pocket. "This is a mess, ladies. All of you should get out of here. Mrs. Sheridan, I am going to pretend like I didn't see you throw something at our mayor. Just leave, ladies."

That night, Jack called Meghan to make sure she arrived

home after the protests. "It just turned to chaos after Mrs. Sheridan threw the tomato," he said to her as she laughed.

"I shouldn't be laughing, but watching Mrs. Sheridan hit her target was too funny," Meghan said.

Jack was silent.

"What's wrong, Jack?" she asked.

Jack sighed. "We received some new information today," he told Meghan. "New information that we believe relates to the dead man."

Meghan gasped. "What? What did you find out?"

"Remember when I was speaking with Jamie about the gun that went missing? Well, we found it, Meghan. We found the missing gun. You won't *believe* where we found it...or better yet, *who* we found it on."

10

"He framed my son for a burglary he never committed twenty-five years ago. If *he* hadn't framed my son, my sweet, precious boy never would have started his own life of crime. That man should be locked up immediately!" Lou wailed as she sat in Jack's office.

Meghan glanced over at Jack and grimaced. She had rushed over to the police station to hear more about the stolen guns, but when she arrived in Jack's office, she had been surprised to find Lou there. Lou, who apparently knew the man who had been caught with the stolen gun, was distraught, and Meghan was concerned that Lou might be on the verge of a heart attack with how upset she seemed.

"I just don't understand," Lou fretted to Jack. "The man with the stolen gun? Did he kill my son or not? Was my son's death a *murder*? I don't understand, Detective Irvin!"

"There, there, Lou," Meghan said softly as she kneeled down beside her. "You need to calm down, Lou. You are going to upset yourself."

"I am already upset," Lou wailed as she buried her face in

her hands. "I was called to this town to identify my son's body and to pick up his things, and now, I find out that the very same man who framed him all of those years ago *might* be responsible for his death? You bet I am upset, Meghan!"

Lou began weeping, and Meghan pulled the old woman in for a hug. "You should give us a few minutes," Meghan mouthed to Jack as he nodded.

"Don't you go," Lou screeched as Jack walked to the door. "I still have questions. When will you know for sure if that scoundrel killed my son? I want answers, Detective Irvin."

Jack sighed. "It might be a few days," Jack said slowly. "The gun will have to be sent off to our forensics lab to see if the residue on the gun matches the residue we found on your son's body."

Lou nodded. "How long should that take?"

Jack shrugged. "At least three or four days, I think. For now, while we investigate the suspect, we would like you to stay in town, Lou. It sounds like you have some valuable information on his prior connection to your son, and I would like to speak more with you."

Lou agreed to stay, and Meghan offered to escort her back to her hotel. "Let's get you home," she said quietly. "You've had a long day, Lou, and I'm sure this news didn't help. I can't believe your son was framed for burglary. How terrible for you, and for him."

"He was a good boy until that happened," Lou explained. "He was sixteen, and the man who framed him—Donald, I believe his name was—stumbled upon my son at the wrong time. My son was arrested, and Donald never came forward with the truth. He even became a police officer—the irony of it. Anyway, I'm not surprised this happened. Donald was a liar all of those years ago, and I'm sure he killed my son."

"I'm so sorry," Meghan whispered as she hugged Lou. "Let's get you back to the hotel. You must be *exhausted*."

Meghan helped Lou rise from her chair. She gently took Lou by the elbow and guided her out of Jack's office, but before they could exit the police station, a tall, burly man pushed by them.

"Hey!" Meghan exclaimed as the man brushed by. "Excuse you."

Lou's eyes widened, and her jaw dropped as she stared up at the man. "You!"

The man stared down at Lou. "Can I help you?"

Lou nodded and began to hit the man. "You framed my son! It's you! You did it, Donald! And now, you've gone and killed him!"

Jack threw himself between Lou and Donald. "Whoa there, folks," he said in alarm. "Let's not cause a ruckus. Donald? You should not be roaming the halls."

Donald glared at Jack. "I haven't been formally arrested yet," he hissed. "I'm a cop. I know my rights. I was talking with Chief Nunan and needed to use the bathroom. I'm free to do that."

Lou stared at Donald, her hands clenching into two tight fists. "I know you killed him," Lou insisted. "I know it!"

Donald shook his head. "I didn't kill anyone," he said with annoyance. "I had nothing to do with that guy dying, and if I hear one more word about it, someone is going to be *sorry*."

11

I t was the evening of the town hall meeting, and Meghan could hardly hear herself think as the crowds of angry people raged in the auditorium of the courthouse. There were people with signs, people with buttons, and people chanting as the police prepared the stage for the Mayor to enter the room.

"Do you think it's going to get ugly?" Meghan whispered to Mrs. Sheridan as they took their spot amidst the other pro-festival protesters.

"I think it might," she replied as Meghan peered around the room. She saw Jack standing in the corner, his walkie-talkie pressed to his ear, and she hoped everyone would be peaceful despite the animosity between the two opposing groups.

"Good evening, everyone," Mayor Rose greeted the audience as he entered the auditorium through a side door. Half of the audience cheered emphatically, while the other half booed.

"Once again, good evening. I want to thank you all for coming out tonight," Mayor Rose announced as he acknowledged the audience. "This has been a difficult week for Sandy Bay, and I am thrilled that we can all come together like this to share our thoughts and feelings."

"I have a *lot* to share with you, Mayor Rose!" Kirsty Fisher declared as she pumped her fist, the string of pearls around her neck becoming lopsided as she waved her arms.

"That's enough for now, Kirsty," Mayor Rose replied. "We are going to do this in an organized way. We will be going around from person to person to share. If you have nothing to share, that is fine, but we will stay here all night until every single person who wants to speak is heard. We will begin on the dissenters' side. Let's see… Ryan Carroll? Ryan, I see you over there. We will begin with you."

Meghan watched as Jack delivered a portable microphone to a rugged-looking man wearing a pair of shabby overalls. He had a thick, brown mustache, which he twirled with his fingers as Jack helped him turn on the microphone.

"Mr. Carroll, please begin," Mayor Rose said as Jack indicated the microphone was on.

"This should be good," Mrs. Sheridan whispered to Meghan. "Ryan Carroll is a chicken farmer from the outskirts of town. He *rarely* shows up at Sandy Bay events, so I can't wait to hear what's got his overalls in a twist about this."

Meghan stifled a giggle as Mrs. Sheridan grinned at her. "You are terrible," she murmured to her.

"Mr. Carroll?" Mayor Rose urged.

Ryan Carroll cleared his throat and began. "I am against continuing this festival," he announced to the crowd in a gruff voice. "The festival brings in rough crowds every year, and it just seems like something bad always happens at that time of year!"

Mayor Rose nodded. "Can you explain a bit more, Mr. Carroll?"

Ryan continued. "Last year, my wife got real sick during the festival," he said.

"That has nothing to do with this," Mrs. Sheridan hissed. "He is just being superstitious, and we are going to lose the festival because of ridiculous claims like this."

The Mayor took down some notes. "Anything else?"

"Yes. This year, on the day of the fireworks, something was in my chicken coop; I heard a loud noise and went outside with my gun and shot at it. I think it was a fox. By the time I got over there, it was gone, but it was just another bad omen."

"Thank you for your contribution, Mr. Carroll," the Mayor said. "Alright, folks. Who is next?"

"I want to speak," Jamie Winston called out. "I have some things to say."

Jamie was given the microphone. He cleared his throat. "I do not agree with Mr. Carroll!" he yelled. "We have to keep this festival. I was able to employ twelve Sandy Bay kids who've been without work for many months to help out at my stand. We had a safety expert ensure that activities at my stand were compliant with all state laws. Everyone who came to my stand enjoyed themselves, and everyone who comes to the Sandy Bay end of year festival always has something great to say about it. It needs to continue!"

The meeting continued for another three hours. As promised, everyone who wanted to speak was granted an audience with the Mayor, and by the time the group was dismissed, it was nearly two in the morning.

"I cannot believe it ran this long," Meghan muttered. "Perhaps if *you* hadn't spoken for forty-five minutes, we could have gotten out of there ages ago, Mrs. Sheridan."

Mrs. Sheridan rolled her eyes. "I'm passionate, Meghan, and I won't let you dampen my enthusiasm. I had a lot to say about keeping the festival going, and I am not ashamed that I let my voice be heard. Besides, you can sleep when you're dead."

Meghan yawned. "You were certainly passionate," she laughed as she recounted Mrs. Sheridan's fiery rant. "I think the Mayor was stunned."

Mrs. Sheridan scoffed. "He didn't even come to a resolution," she complained. "His little speech about Sandy Bay coming together and uniting as a town was too vague. I want answers, and he did not give them. Is the festival continuing or not? Do I need to tie myself to a tree with a sign and protest? Do I need to hold a hunger strike? Do I need to show someone how old Sally Sheridan can use her cane? I need answers."

Meghan pursed her lips. "I thought the Mayor's speech at the end was nice," she admitted. "I think the people of Sandy Bay need to come together. All of this tension is terrible for the town, and if we don't fix things soon, friendships could be broken. Families could split. I would hate to see this blow up into something bigger than it has become, you know?"

Mrs. Sheridan thought for a moment, furrowing her brow. "I don't know, Meghan," she said. "I think until the police figure out exactly what happened to that guy who died, things are going to be in turmoil. I just have a bad feeling about all of this, and I can't put my finger on what it is."

1 2

The next morning, Meghan closed the bakery for a much-needed day off. "It'll be good for both of us," Meghan chirped to Trudy on the phone.

"What are you going to do today?" Trudy asked.

"Jack and I are going fishing with our dogs," she told Trudy with excitement. "I've never been fishing, and my little dogs and Dash, Jack's dog, love playing together. It'll be a fun day out."

When Jack picked Meghan up, she could tell that something was on his mind. His blue eyes looked cold and distant, and as Meghan went in to kiss him, he pulled away. "What is the matter?" Meghan asked Jack. "Everything okay?"

Jack nodded. "I'm sorry," he said as he pulled Meghan into a tight hug. "I'm trying to figure out some new pieces of information about this case. I didn't mean to be rude."

"It's fine," she replied as she gently kissed Jack on the cheek. "I'm sorry this case has been such a doozy."

Jack helped Meghan into his truck. He fastened Fiesta and Siesta into their crate and then began driving toward the little lake on the edge of town.

"This will be fun," Meghan declared as she smiled at Jack. "A day off with *you* is just what I needed."

Despite his apology, Meghan saw Jack was still preoccupied. His mind was elsewhere, and after trying to force the conversation, Meghan gave up and looked out the window. She could see the Pacific Ocean in the distance, and she shivered as she imagined how cold the water must be.

Jack parked the truck near a little grove. He removed the fishing equipment from the back as Meghan released the dogs from their crates. "They're having a good time already," she said as he walked silently toward the water.

As Jack attached a worm to the end of his fishing line, Meghan sat down beside him and stared into his eyes. "What?" he asked.

Meghan sighed. "You've been off today," she told him. "I feel like you don't want me here."

Jack shook his head. "No," he said. "I'm so sorry, Meghan. I don't want to make you feel that way. I'm just so wrapped up in this case. It feels like there have been so many twists and turns, and I'm looking for answers as hard as I can so that the town can quiet down again."

Meghan squeezed Jack's hand. "It's been a wild time in this town, that's for sure."

Jack leaned over and put his head on Meghan's shoulder. "I'm just ready for a break."

Meghan touched Jack's cheek. "I have a crazy idea," she giggled as Jack looked out at the still water. "What if that farmer from the town hall shot him? He said he thought he shot a fox. Or what if it was someone who had attended Jamie's gun show exhibition? What if this was all some big accident?"

Jack's jaw dropped. He pulled away from Meghan and rose to his feet. "Meghan," he said slowly. "That might be the most valuable suggestion anyone has made regarding this case."

Meghan shook her head. "Jack, that was a joke," she replied. "Come on, babe. I was just kidding."

Jack's blue eyes widened. "Meghan," he responded. "We have to go. Call the dogs right now. We'll come back for the supplies later."

Two hours later, Meghan sat outside of Jack's office for what felt like the millionth time that week. "If I have to sit in this police station for one more hour...." Meghan muttered to herself as she brushed a stray strand of dark hair from her eyes.

The door opened and Jack stepped outside. "Is everything okay?" she asked.

Jack nodded. "Ryan Carroll is telling me all about the gun he used to shoot what he believed was a fox," Jack told Meghan. "He's been very forthcoming; I'm glad we brought him in."

Meghan's eyes widened. "Does he have any more information?"

Jack grinned. "I think he might," he told Meghan. "I need to run and fetch Chief Nunan, but I promise, I'll be done here within the hour."

Meghan watched as Jack scurried down the corridor. She was brimming with curiosity; what had Ryan Carroll revealed to Jack? She had only thrown out his name to make Jack laugh; it was ridiculous to think that Ryan could have shot that man and not known it, and Meghan was sure that it had been silly to abandon their fishing trip. Still, Meghan could not contain her curiosity. She looked around, and when she saw no one, she slipped inside of Jack's office to find Ryan Carroll sitting in a thin wooden chair.

"I don't believe we've met," Meghan said as she extended her right hand. "I'm Meghan Truman. I'm rather new to

Sandy Bay, and I own the bakery. Nice to meet you, Mr. Carroll."

Ryan Carroll stared at Meghan. "It's real nice to meet you," he said. "I'm real nervous being down here at the station. I don't really know why I'm here. Detective Irvin has been asking all sorts of questions about the night that man died, and I don't know why. I wasn't even at the festival that night. I was in bed long before that man died; as soon as I took care of the fox in the chicken coop out back, I went right to sleep."

Meghan smiled at Ryan. "Don't be nervous," she assured him. "Jack—Detective Irvin—is a good, fair guy. He'll make sure everything is okay. He just has to ask questions sometimes. It's his job."

Suddenly, the door burst open. Jack and Chief Nunan both entered the room, each with a file folder in their hands.

"Meghan, you shouldn't be in here," Jack warned. "Please leave. We need to discuss something of great importance immediately."

Meghan slipped out of the office, but she did not leave. Instead, she pressed her right ear firmly against the door to Jack's office to eavesdrop.

"From our reports on the gun that killed the deceased," Chief Nunan began. "The gun that was stolen from Jamie Winston's shop did *not* kill that man; Donald will be charged for stealing the gun, but he will *not* be charged for murder."

Meghan heard silence, and her heart began to pound. "Why are you telling me this?" Ryan asked Chief Nunan. "Who is Donald?"

Jack cleared his throat. "We are telling you this because after our initial reports from the coroner and from our forensics office, it is abundantly clear that the man at the festival died because of a wound—wound from a shotgun."

Meghan heard Ryan gasp. "A shotgun?" he sputtered.

"Yes, a shotgun." Chief Nunan answered.

"You wouldn't happen to have shot a shotgun at approximately seven at night on the last night of the festival, would you have?" Jack asked Ryan. "Perhaps to shoot a fox?"

Ryan did not answer, and she heard a loud crash from inside Jack's office. "Detective Irvin," Chief Nunan said calmly. "I need you to call the paramedics immediately. It appears that Mr. Carroll has passed out."

Two weeks later, life had finally returned to normal in Sandy Bay. The protests had finally ended after Mayor Rose had decided to keep the fall festival going, but to add more security, and everyone had returned to their formerly friendly, hospitable selves.

The big news in town was the true cause of death for Lou's son. After interviewing Ryan Carroll and performing a forensics report on his shotgun, Jack and the Sandy Bay Police Department had concluded that Ryan *had* shot the man. Upon reviewing security footage from the festival, as well as CCTV footage from Ryan's farm, he was found to be innocent; the death was ruled accidental, and while Ryan was devastated, he was allowed to walk free as an innocent man.

"It's nice to have some peace and quiet around here," Meghan cooed as she poured a cup of steaming coffee for Jack at the bakery. "Between that police officer from out of town being caught with the stolen gun from Jamie's shop, to Lou's son's death, to Ryan's shock over the matter, it's been a wild few weeks."

"Meghan? Meghan, can we chat?"

Meghan bit her bottom lip as Karen walked into the dining area. "Trudy let me come in through the back…." Karen said as she lowered her eyes.

"What's up, Karen?" Meghan said cooly, still taken aback by her friend's behavior during the protests.

"I'm sorry it's taken me so long to make it in," she said softly. "I'm embarrassed, Meghan, and I have hardly been able to even walk by the bakery. I was so rude to you about the protests, and I should have behaved better…"

Meghan saw the sadness in Karen's eyes, and she walked to her friend and hugged her. "Karen," she murmured. "You are my dearest friend in Sandy Bay. I never want anything to come between us."

Karen nodded. "I know! I let a silly event get to my head, and I treated you terribly. Can you forgive me? I miss you, Meghan, and I'm sorry it's taken me two weeks to come around and apologize."

Meghan smiled. "It doesn't matter how long it took you; to me, it's the thought that counts. I am so happy to see you, Karen, and I hope you know that there is no bad blood between us."

Karen wiped a happy tear from her eyes and kissed Meghan on the cheek. As she turned to leave, she looked at Jack. "Jack Irvin," she said. "I hope you know what a gem you have here. Meghan is a doll, and if you don't know that, you'll have to answer to me!"

Jack laughed. "Oh, I know it, Karen," he replied playfully. "I know it."

Karen waved goodbye, and Meghan turned back to Jack. "That was a surprise. You just never know who or what will come through the doors of my bakery."

Meghan and Jack's heads turned as the little silver bells on the door chimed. Jacqueline walked in, her face aglow. "Meghan, you are just who I wanted to see."

Meghan giggled. "See what I mean?" Meghan said to Jack. "You just never know what's going to happen at Truly Sweet."

Jack stood up. "Should I leave you two alone?"

Jacqueline shook her head. "No, this is all good news, Detective Irvin. Meghan, remember what you told me a few weeks ago? To work hard and keep believing in myself? Well, I decided to have a better attitude about my salon, and my business has nearly doubled. I just tried to make every little interaction with my clients count, and I think it's working. Meghan, you are such a good role model for me as a businesswoman, and I wanted to thank you for your encouragement."

Meghan gasped as Jacqueline pulled a card and a bouquet of sunflowers from her purse. "For me?" she asked.

"Yes," Jacqueline told her. "To you, from me. I hope you will forgive me for being rude a few weeks ago. Just know that I really look up to you, and I hope we can be better friends."

Meghan's heart warmed. "I hope that too," she told Jacqueline as Jacqueline turned to leave.

"What a day for you," Jack told Meghan as she admired her flowers. "You are incredible, Meghan. You have been such a light in this town."

"I wouldn't say that," she protested.

"I would."

Lou walked into the bakery with a thin smile on her face. "It's good to see you both. Detective Irvin, Meghan, how are you both?"

Meghan rushed over to Lou and hugged her. "Oh Lou," she began. "It is so good to see you. I hope you are doing okay?"

Lou nodded. "Learning the truth about my son's death has really put this mother's heart at ease," she informed

Meghan. "And learning that Donald will be in jail for stealing that gun? Well, that was just a little extra good news. Anyway, I am leaving town to return home, but I had to stop by and thank you for being so kind during my time here."

Meghan kissed Lou's cheek. "You deserve all the kindness in the world," she said to Lou. "I am just glad I could be helpful to you."

Lou embraced Meghan. "You were such a pleasant person to run into," she whispered. "I hope we can keep in touch."

Meghan nodded. "Of course. I would love that, Lou."

Lou smiled warmly. "Well, then I will hope to hear from you soon. Goodbye, Detective. Goodbye, Meghan."

As Lou walked out of the bakery, Jack pulled Meghan close to him. He closed his eyes and leaned down, kissing Meghan tenderly on the lips. Meghan sighed, enjoying the moment.

"Like I said, you are a light in this town," Jack murmured to Meghan as he gently pulled away. "Two people came by to thank you for your kindness today! I hope you realize how wonderful you are."

Meghan fluttered her eyelashes at Jack. "You are too much, Jack."

Jack shook his head. "We are lucky to have you here, Meghan. Sandy Bay is so very lucky to have Meghan Truman, and I hope you know I feel very lucky as well."

Meghan blushed, feeling her body grow warm. "Jack," she said slowly. "I feel like the lucky one here. My life is truly sweet in Sandy Bay, and I wouldn't have things any other way."

The End

ICE CREAM AND GUILTY
PLEASURES

ABOUT ICE CREAM AND GUILTY PLEASURES

Released: November, 2018
Series: Book 9 – Sandy Bay Cozy Mystery Series
Standalone: Yes
Cliff-hanger: No

Meghan Truman is honored to be invited to serve her signature tarts at the Governor's ball. A night of glitz and glamour, in the company of handsome Detective Jack Irvin, is ruined for her when she experiences firsthand, the ungracious attitude of a prominent figure that she once looked up to.

Things take a turn for the worse when this insolent guest is found dead after eating a dish of ice cream. Meghan is sure she had nothing to do with it as her desserts were rejected by the deceased.

Will Megan and Jack be able to navigate this unfamiliar world of wealth and privilege to discover the truth in time to save her business?

Not all sweet things are pleasurable.

The guilty can sometimes be sweet.

Discover how Meghan helps to solve the latest murder mystery in Sandy Bay.

1

I t was a snowy night in Sandy Bay, and as Meghan Truman snuggled beneath a patterned wool blanket, she felt like the luckiest girl in the world. Her new friend, Jacqueline, had invited her over for some television and girl talk while her boyfriend, Jack, had taken her out the night before to *Luciano's*, her favorite Italian restaurant in town.

"That was such a good show," Jacqueline gushed as the light from the fireplace made her eyes glow. "Let's flip over to the news; we've been watching so much of this reality show that I think my brain is turning to mush!"

"Oh, stop," Meghan protested good-naturedly. "Miss-to-Mrs. has been my favorite show since college. The contestants are so funny and ridiculous, and it's hilarious to watch them compete for one fellow's attention."

Jacqueline playfully stuck out her tongue and rose from her position on the couch. "While you watch the end of this silly show, I'm going to go grab another glass of cabernet for you. I know it's one you like, and you'll need a little wine when we switch over to a serious news show as opposed to this goofy trash TV."

Meghan chuckled as Jacqueline walked into the kitchen. "Make sure it's a small pour," she called to her. "It's my favorite drink, but I have a lot of things to do tomorrow. I'm busy at the bakery this weekend, and I have so many errands to do."

Jacqueline wrinkled her nose as she walked back into her dimly lit living room with two glasses of red wine in her hands. "Trudy agreed to a three-day weekend? That's probably for the best for *both* of you...you did say that she's been a little moody lately."

Meghan nodded as she thought of her assistant. Trudy had been a helpful companion at the bakery for a few months, but lately, she had been fussy and irritable, and Meghan was eager to get some time away from her.

"Well anyway, here is your cabernet," Jacqueline said as she handed the glass to Meghan. "I hope you like it."

Meghan took a sip and sighed. "It's perfect," she cooed as she passed the remote to Jacqueline. "I *guess* you can change the channel now, *Jackie*."

Jacqueline laughed. "Hardly anyone calls me Jackie, but I like it. It's cute."

Meghan grinned. "Jackie it is, then." She settled back against the couch and yawned. "I'm getting sleepy. I'm afraid the news will just knock me right out."

Jacqueline shrugged, but as she changed the channel to the Sandy Bay News station, both women gasped. "Look at that," she murmured as the sight of dozens of elegantly dressed couples filled the screen. The couples paraded around an ornate ballroom, and then the show flashed to a shot of ten smiling people being served lobster on gold plates.

"What is this? More reality television?" Meghan asked in

wonder as her dark eyes widened. "This is the Sandy Bay News channel, isn't it? Surely something so fancy isn't happening in Sandy Bay?"

Jackie raised a finger to her lips. "Shhhhh," she ordered Meghan. "I want to hear what this is."

The channel cut to a shot of a young, stunningly beautiful brunette woman reporting from a studio. She had a dazzling white smile, and her eyes twinkled as she addressed the audience. "With the upcoming Governor's Ball around the corner, there is no doubt that this event will be the social event of the year in Sandy Bay. We just showed you clips from last year's event, and as a reporter *and* guest, I can say that it was a fine affair. With celebrities coming into Sandy Bay from around the world, a marvelous menu, and a live band, the Governor's Ball is a night to remember. Isn't that right, Kirsty?"

Meghan's jaw dropped. "Of course Kirsty Fisher is in charge of such a fancy event," she muttered as Kirsty Fisher, one of Sandy Bay's social butterflies, appeared next to the young brunette woman. As a business owner in Sandy Bay, Meghan had frequently interacted with Kirsty who was constantly trying to get her to help with events in town, or provide goods for a party or festival, and while Meghan admired Kirsty's commitment to her causes, she could be a bit much.

"Thank you for having me," Kirsty smiled as she flipped her blonde hair behind her narrow shoulders. "This year's ball will be the night of all nights! We have so many special guests coming to town, and of course, Governor Brown and his lovely wife, Paula, will be hosting. The tickets are five-thousand dollars per person this year, and the planning committee is delighted to see how much fun we can have. Come, everyone. Purchase tickets before they sell out!"

Meghan clapped her hands in delight. "Jackie, Paula

Brown is from Texas, my home state. She was Miss Texas years ago, and then she became an actress in Hollywood. She is *so* beautiful. I grew up with a picture of her on the wall in my bedroom."

Jackie smiled. "That's adorable, Meghan. Maybe you can sneak into the Governor's Ball and meet her?"

Meghan raised an eyebrow. "I would *have* to sneak in," she admitted. "I cannot afford a five-thousand dollar ticket to the ball. Maybe someday…"

The television screen turned to black, and then it revealed a middle-aged man in a white chef's hat. "Look at that, Meghan," Jackie said as she pointed to the screen. "It's Claude Boucher. He's that famous chef from Paris. He *must* be in town as a celebrity guest at the ball."

"I *know* who Claude Boucher is," Meghan boasted. "I *do* own a bakery. Claude Boucher is one of the most famous chefs and bakers in the world right now."

The two women watched as Claude sat across from a red-headed reporter on a green leather couch. "Mr. Boucher," the reporter asked. "You will be a guest at the ball this year, but a little bird tells me that you are assisting the planning committee in designing the menu? What can you tell us about this?"

Claude leaned back and brushed the silver hair from his forehead. He smiled, and Meghan noticed the deep dimples in his cheeks. "Well, it is an honor to design the menu," Claude declared as he crossed his right leg over his left leg. "And unlike other years, we are not going to be exclusively importing the foods from France."

The red-headed reporter leaned in. "Oh? So this year will be different? Where will the foods be found for the Governor's Ball?"

Claude gestured at the camera. "From here, of course. We are celebrating local foods this year to give the Governor's

Ball just a little something special. For example, we usually fly in our crème brûlée from Paris, but this year, we have been investigating local options from the Pacific Northwest."

Meghan's heart began pounding in her chest. "Jackie," she whispered as Claude flashed a radiant smile to the red-headed reporter. "Jackie, they're asking *local* chefs and bakers to cater the Governor's Ball. *I'm* a local baker!"

Jackie jerked her chin at the television. "Be quiet. We need details, lady."

As Meghan shut her mouth, Claude grinned. "We've been quietly searching up and down the West Coast for the best of *all* dining options, and I am thrilled to say that for this year, we have chosen the Truly Sweet bakery in Sandy Bay to provide the desserts for the Governor's Ball."

Meghan fell off of the couch. "Jackie," she murmured with a shaking voice. "Jackie, he just said Truly Sweet. He just announced that *my* bakery is going to be providing the desserts for the biggest event of the year."

Jackie ran over to Meghan and wrapped her arms around her. "This is fantastic news. I cannot believe this. You should be so proud."

As the two women embraced, Meghan's heart fluttered with joy. She closed her eyes and imagined her night at the Governor's Ball. She had been to fine events before, but never something as prestigious as this one. As Jackie began to squeal in celebration, Meghan felt a happy tear roll down her cheek.

"This is just truly sweet, Jackie," Meghan exclaimed as she wiped the tear from her dark eyes. "This news is truly sweet!"

2

"Pamela, you are doing a wonderful job," Meghan gushed as she watched her newest employee drizzle hazelnut icing atop a freshly baked tart. "You have caught on to Truly Sweet's treat-making processes so quickly. I am *quite* impressed."

Pamela beamed at Meghan, her braces shining in the light of the sunny afternoon. Meghan had hired the teenager the previous week to do some cleaning in the evenings, but after Meghan had caught her frosting a cake like an expert, she knew that Pamela had talent and should be promoted.

"The way you fluffed the dough earlier was lovely, and I saw you added three cups of butter to the mix. I usually only add one and a half cups of butter, but after trying your batch of tarts, I think I need to add more."

Pamela's brown eyes glittered. "I've been practicing, Meghan. Making these tarts for you was so much fun, and I just want to keep baking and baking and baking."

Trudy stormed into the kitchen, her greying hair messy and her clothes covered in flour. "Meghan, the dishes are done and the cookies have been baked. May I go, now?"

Meghan nodded. "Sure, Trudy," she said as Trudy walked to the door. "No problem."

Pamela turned to look at Meghan. "What's her problem? I feel like she doesn't like me."

Meghan shook her head. "It's not you," she assured her as she ran a hand through her long, dark hair. "Trudy's been in a weird funk lately. Don't take it personally."

Pamela smiled. "That's what my soccer coach says when the other team is rude. It isn't wise to take things personally from people who do not know us personally."

Meghan grinned. "You are wise for an eighteen-year-old," she told her. "It's nice having you around. You remind me a bit of Lori, one of the girls who used to help me here."

Before Pamela could respond, the yellow door of the bakery flew open, sending the little bells attached to the door flying about. Claude Boucher strutted into the bakery, and Meghan nearly dropped the long, plastic tube she was using to ice the tarts. "Bonjour," Claude called out as he smiled at Meghan and Pamela. "I hope I am not interrupting anything important."

Meghan's mouth was agape, and she could not form a coherent thought. She remembered Claude's appearance on the news the previous week, and the announcement that her bakery had been chosen to provide the treats for the ball, but after hearing nothing, she had forgotten about the excitement. Now, as Claude stood before her in her bakery, Meghan's face grew red, and her hands began to shake.

"We're just finishing these tarts," Pamela informed Claude as she handed him one. "Would you like to try one? I modified the recipe, but Meghan says they are some of the best she has ever had."

Claude looked from Pamela to Meghan. "I would love to sample one of the tarts, but first, I must know who is the owner of this quaint little bakery? Where can I find the proprietor?"

Meghan stuttered, unable to maintain her composure around the famous chef. "It's… it's… it's…"

"It's her," Pamela said matter-of-factly as she pointed to Meghan. "She owns the bakery. I just started helping out last week."

Claude reached for Meghan's right hand and drew it to his lips. A chill ran down Meghan's spine as he kissed her hand, and she could feel her cheeks growing warm. "Meghan Truman, it is truly a pleasure to make your acquaintance. No one told me how lovely you would be, and I am so happy to finally meet you."

Meghan stared at Claude. "Nice… nice… nice… to… nice to…"

Pamela looked confusedly at Meghan, and then she took Claude's hand. "Meghan is happy to meet you, and so I am. You have an accent. Where are you from?"

Claude graciously smiled at Pamela. "I am from Paris. I am a chef there, young lady, and from the looks of things, you are a little chef as well."

Pamela grinned. "I help Meghan here with odds and ends, but I hope to be doing more baking in the future. For now, though, I am late for soccer practice. Meghan, I'll see you tomorrow."

Meghan stared as Pamela tore off her soiled apron and dashed out of the front door. Claude returned his attention to Meghan and grinned. "Meghan Truman, I have some very exciting news for you. Have you heard of the Governor's Ball? It is the premiere event in the Pacific Northwest."

Meghan nodded, still struggling to speak, but Claude continued, "this year, we are sourcing our catering from local vendors," he explained to her. "We have searched near and far, and the planning committee has decided that your bakery will be providing desserts for the event, if you are open to the idea. Kirsty Fisher spoke very highly of you, and after reading the excellent reviews you have received after only months of your business being open, we cannot pass up the opportunity to work with you. What do you say? Will you provide the desserts for the ball, Meghan? Oh, say yes!"

Meghan nodded enthusiastically. "Yes," she told Claude, thankful that she at least could manage to answer the most important question she had been asked in her professional career. "Yes."

"Very good," Claude declared as he snatched her hand and planted another kiss on it. "With that, I must go. I will be in touch regarding the event. Take care, Meghan."

Before she could process Claude's visit and her good fortune, her tall, handsome boyfriend, Jack, burst into the bakery waving two pieces of paper in the air. "Meghan, I did it," he shouted in delight as he sprinted to where Meghan stood in the middle of the dining room. "Hey, I did it!"

Meghan shook her head, her mind still clouded with the impact of Claude's visit. "What? Jack, what are you talking about? What did you do?"

Jack's blue eyes danced with excitement, and he took Meghan's hands in his. "I scored two tickets to the ball, Meghan. We're going to the Governor's Ball."

Meghan raised an eyebrow. "Are you working security for the event or something?"

Jack shook his head. "No, Meghan," he said as he squeezed her hands. "We're attending the event! This detective is off duty for the ball. I just want a night of fun with my girl, and this is going to be an amazing event."

Meghan pulled her hands from Jack's. "I don't understand," she told him. "The tickets are five-thousand dollars,

Jack. I know you received that promotion a few months ago, but detectives can't afford that kind of ticket. The ball is important; all the proceeds go to charity, but I do not want you to go into a financial hole just to make me happy."

Jack ran a hand through his blonde hair. Meghan could see he was frustrated, and she put a hand on his shoulder. "Jack? Where did you get the tickets?"

"It's fine, Meghan," he assured her. "My former colleague, Michelle, got them for me; she used to work here in town, but now she works in the capital for Governor Brown. She called me up out of the blue and offered the tickets, and how could I say no? A night of dinner and dancing with the most gorgeous girl in Sandy Bay? My answer was yes, and she sent over the tickets today."

Meghan bit her bottom lip. "Are you sure it's okay?" Meghan asked Jack as he crossed his arms across his muscular chest. "It's a pretty big favor, Jack. Those tickets cost a lot of money. Are you sure she doesn't want anything in return?"

Jack frowned. "She's a former professional colleague, Meghan," he told her as she stared into his eyes. "She's doing a nice thing for us, and I think we should *both* be appreciative."

Meghan shrugged. "Well, you can return one of the tickets; I was asked to make the desserts for the event, so I will be given a free spot at the ball."

Jack's jaw dropped. "It's official? They asked you? Meghan, that is amazing. I am so proud of you."

Jack picked Meghan up and spun her around the dining room as she giggled. "It's not a big deal," she protested as Jack kissed her on the cheek.

"It is a big deal," he argued. "We will dine and dance and indulge in your desserts at the ball. I'll send that ticket back over to Mitchelle, but I am so happy I will be able to be there to watch you shine."

Meghan nodded. "It will be a great time," she said as Jack kissed her on the forehead. "My desserts and my boyfriend at the best event this town has seen? What could go wrong?"

3

The morning of the ball, Meghan assembled her team in the dining room of the bakery to go over final preparations. It was only five in the morning, and while Meghan typically did not enjoy rising before the sun, today, she was giddy as she sipped her extra large caramel cappuccino.

"This is the biggest day of my career, everyone," she announced to the sleepy-eyed group. "I cannot thank you enough for volunteering to help me with the Governor's Ball."

"I'm your employee, Meghan. I didn't quite volunteer," Trudy grumbled.

Meghan ignored Trudy's insolent tone and continued, "Your help is so appreciated. You will be partnering with Claude's team to prepare our desserts at the event, and it will be the night of a lifetime. His team flew in last night from Paris, and I'm sure they will have a lot of tips and tricks we can learn."

Pamela grinned. "I can't believe we're going to work with people from Paris tonight. This is going to be the best."

"It will be," Meghan agreed. "Pamela, I have let Claude's team know you'll be assisting with the tarts; they seem to be your specialty, and I'm thrilled to see what you'll create tonight."

Pamela gave Meghan a playful salute. "Aye aye, Captain Meghan. Happy to assist where the Captain orders."

Meghan turned to Trudy. "The team knows you're my top assistant," she explained. "As I'll be seated with the other guests during the event, all questions regarding the desserts from Truly Sweet will be deferred to you."

Trudy frowned. "So while you dance the night away, I'm going to be working in the kitchen to make your treats while you get the credit?"

Meghan shook her head. "No, Trudy. This is a team effort. Truly Sweet would not be where it is today if I didn't have a wonderful group working with me, and I hope you know how grateful I am for your help."

Trudy mumbled under her breath, and Meghan stifled the urge to say something snarky. She didn't understand why her assistant had been so disgruntled lately, but she hoped Trudy would soon return to her normal, chipper self.

"Credit or no credit, I'm just happy to be here," Pamela declared as Trudy rolled her eyes.

Meghan ruffled Pamela's short blonde hair. "I love your excitement, Pamela, and to further the excitement, I have a surprise for all of you."

Meghan disappeared into the kitchen, returning with two large purple garment bags. She gave one to Pamela and one to Trudy. "As the ball is going to be a night to remember, I thought that the Truly Sweet team deserved to look their best. Open your bags, ladies."

Pamela tore open her garment bag and began to shriek. "It's gorgeous, Meghan. Look at this outfit! I'll look like a proper chef in this. Meghan, thank you, thank you, thank you."

Meghan smiled. She had specially ordered the yellow chef smocks from her favorite online boutique; each was trimmed with lace, and Trudy and Pamela's initials were embroidered in large, elegant cursive on the left side. With bell sleeves and tiny white buttons that studded both sides of the coat, the smocks had been expensive, but with chefs and bakers flying in from France, Meghan wanted her crew to look like professionals.

"They're nice," Trudy admitted as she ran her hands over the long smock. "But we'll ruin them will the flour and sugar. Seems like a waste of good money to me."

Meghan pasted a grin on her face. "I was happy to buy them. I think you'll both look beautiful. So, Pamela? You will be helping with the tarts, and Trudy, you are essentially in charge. I'll be nearby if either of you need anything, though, so there should be no issues."

Pamela stood up to hug Meghan. "Thanks, boss," Pamela said as she embraced Meghan. "I'll be there right on time."

Trudy nodded at Meghan as she walked to the door. "See you later, Meghan."

Twelve hours later, Meghan took one last look at herself in the mirror as she applied a layer of mauve lipstick that matched the floor-length ballgown that her dear friend, Karen, had advised her to pick up from her house earlier.

"It was mine as a young woman," Karen informed Meghan as she nervously clutched the phone. "The color is fantastic, and the style is timeless. You'll be a dream in it."

"I hope you're right," Meghan sighed as she glanced over at the dress she had originally chosen. During her late morning shower, her little twin dogs, Fiesta and Siesta, had gotten sick on the dress, and by the time Meghan realized it, it was far too late to send it to the dry-cleaner. She had frantically called Karen, who was away on holiday, and as per usual, she had saved the day.

The ballgown fit Meghan like a glove; the sweetheart neckline accentuated her shoulders and collarbone, and a simple diamond pendant rested just beneath her neck.

The empress waist hit Meghan's curves in all the right places; she was sometimes self-conscious about her womanly figure, but tonight, she felt like a princess as she smiled at her reflection. The color of the dress made her olive skin glow, and her long dark hair was pinned back into a sophisticated chignon.

"Wow," Meghan heard Jack say from behind her. She spun around to find him staring at her in the doorway of her bedroom.

"Jack, I didn't even hear you come in," Meghan said as she stared at her boyfriend. "You frightened me."

He walked to Meghan and kissed her softly on the lips. "You look stunning, Meghan," Jack whispered as he wrapped his arms around her waist. "That dress... that wasn't the one you first picked, was it?"

Meghan pulled back from his embrace and spun around, the ballgown's many layers ruffling loudly. "The dogs ruined my other dress," she admitted. "This was a last minute save from Karen. It was Karen's dress from when she was young. I was a little worried that it would be out of style; she is in her seventies, and fashion was different back then."

Jack shook his head. "It's perfect. I've never seen you look so lovely."

Meghan looked at Jack and gave a silly whistle. "You don't look too bad yourself, Detective Irvin," Meghan murmured as she leaned in to kiss Jack's cheek. "You're quite dapper in that tuxedo, my dear."

"Well, sweetheart, I had to look nice for my lady," Jack announced as he gave his elbow to Meghan. She slipped her arm into his, and they walked downstairs, Meghan careful not to trip on the hem of her skirts.

"I'll get the door for you," Jack told Meghan as he helped her into his car. "Let's go, Meghan."

Meghan settled into the car, eager to see what the Governor's Ball had in store for her for and her bakery. "I'm so excited," she said. "Between my desserts being served, you looking so handsome, and rubbing elbows with Paula Brown, the former Miss Texas, I believe that tonight will be a fairytale."

"As do I," he replied. "It was so awesome that Michelle got the ticket for me."

Meghan bit her lip. "Yeah," she responded. "So awesome."

"Michelle is great," Jack gushed as he drove toward the Sandy Bay Event Hall. "Her job is so cool, too. Her transition from the police force to the Governor's staff was seamless, it seemed; she's risen through the ranks so easily. I hope I can do that someday. I'd love to work for the governor, and it would be so fun to work with Michelle again. She's the best."

Meghan furrowed her brow. "I bet it would," she said, irritated that on her big night, her boyfriend was singing the praises of another woman.

"What?" Jack asked as he looked over at Meghan. "What's the matter?"

Meghan shook her head. "Nothing. It's just annoying that on the night I dress up like a movie star, the biggest night of my career, you're telling me all about another woman."

Jack laughed, but then seeing the serious look on Meghan's face, he stopped. "Are you serious? Meghan, Michelle is my friend."

Meghan shrugged. "I've never heard of her, and she got a five-thousand dollar ticket for you. That seems a little too friendly to me."

Jack narrowed his eyes at Meghan. "I wouldn't be coming

to your big night if Michelle hadn't generously given me one of her free tickets," he said as Meghan turned to stare out the window. "You need to relax, Meghan. It's going to be a great night. Don't let this spoil it for you. Michelle is just a friend."

Meghan grimaced. "Whatever you say."

Jack reached over and squeezed Meghan's hand. "Hey," he said. "Seriously, stop looking for reasons to be fussy. It's your big night, Meghan. Nothing is going to stand in the way of you, me, and one heck of a good time, sweetheart."

4

Meghan's dark eyes sparkled as she stepped out of Jack's car and onto the red carpet stretched outside of the Governor's Ball. Jack rushed around to help Meghan, and she slipped her arm through his elbow, forgetting the tense moments they had shared before arriving.

"Look at all the paparazzi," Meghan whispered into Jack's ear as he guided her along the red carpet. "There are reporters here from major news networks. They came all the way to Sandy Bay for the ball. I can't believe this."

"Meghan Truman!"

Meghan glanced over her left shoulder to see a reporter waving at her from behind the metal barrier that separated the press from the guests. "Meghan Truman? Aren't you the owner of the bakery providing the desserts for the event?"

"Yes, she is."

Meghan gasped as Claude snuck up from behind and wrapped an arm around Meghan's waist. Claude nodded at Jack and then grinned down at Meghan. "Beautiful Meghan Truman, it is so lovely to see you here."

"It's so nice to be here," Meghan sputtered as Claude tugged at Meghan's waist to lead her down the red carpet. Jack pulled back, letting Claude take Meghan away. "Smile and wave at the press, Meghan. Give them what they want."

Meghan laughed as Claude struck a pose and blew a kiss at one of the reporters.

"I'll catch up with you, Meghan," Jack called out as Claude and Meghan drew further away. "I'll see you inside," she replied.

Claude dropped his arm from Meghan's waist and took her hand, giving it a squeeze as they walked across the threshold and into the ballroom. "Get ready to be amazed," Claude purred into Meghan's ear. "This will be a night you will never forget."

"He's right," Meghan thought as they stepped into the ballroom and she surveyed the massive, beautifully decorated candle-lit room. "I will *never* forget this night."

Candles glittered on every surface of the room, and the tables were set with gold plates. Displays of red and white roses wound across the railing of the grand staircase in the middle of the ballroom, and ten chandeliers hung from the ceiling. Meghan had never seen such finery before, and while she had seen images from previous balls on the news, the reality of the event was more than she could have ever imagined.

"Come, Meghan," Claude murmured as he adjusted his black bow tie. "I have so many people to introduce you to. Your desserts have already been quite the hit, and there are some fabulous people who want to meet you."

"That would be fantastic," Meghan said as she fluttered her eyelashes.

"Steve! Carol!" Claude called out to a middle-aged couple. "Meghan, this is Steve and his wife, Carol. They are dear friends of mine. Carol owns a talent firm in Los Angeles, and Steve recently retired from a career in hospitality."

"It's a pleasure," Meghan told the couple as she shook their hands.

"The pleasure is ours," Carol cooed. "Your desserts are wonderful; I spoiled my diet to eat some of your tarts, and it was sure worth it."

"Oh, Kenzie, dear," Claude shouted at a young, statuesque blonde woman. "Kenzie, come meet Meghan. Meghan, this is Kenzie. She is a top model in Paris, and she flew in for the event. Kenzie, Meghan is responsible for all the amazing desserts here tonight."

Kenzie leaned forward to kiss Meghan on both cheeks. "Your desserts are divine," she told Meghan in a thick French accent. "Tres magnifque."

Meghan glowed as Claude showed her off to his many friends. "Is there anyone else you would care to meet?" Claude asked as he beamed at Meghan. "I think I have introduced you to nearly everyone I know."

Meghan shook her head, but then she remembered the person she had been aching to meet since she was a little girl. "Actually, there is someone."

"Oh, Meghan," Claude fretted as he looked down at his rose gold cell phone. "It appears there is a little disaster in the kitchen. I must go check on things. Excuse me."

Meghan watched as Claude scurried off. She looked around the room for her boyfriend, but when she did not see Jack, Meghan bit her bottom lip. "I could just stand here alone," Meghan thought to herself. "Or…."

Meghan gathered her skirts in her hands and took off toward the head table. She could see Kirsty Fisher laughing as she sipped a glass of champagne, and just as Meghan hoped, seated right next to Kirsty was Paula Brown.

"Just the woman I want to meet," Meghan said under her

breath as she walked daintily toward the head table. "I can't wait to meet my hero."

She waited until Kirsty and Paula had finished their conversation before she gingerly tapped Paula on the shoulder. "Excuse me? Mrs. Brown?"

Paula Brown scowled as she turned to glare at Meghan. "Can I help you?"

Meghan smiled warmly, but before she could introduce herself, Kirsty spotted her. "Meghan, hello. The desserts are excellent. I am so thrilled that you were able to help with the event. Paula, dear, Meghan here helped with the desserts tonight."

Paula looked up and down and Meghan and then turned back to face Kirsty. "That's nice, but why is she here now? Are you here to take my dessert order or something, Melanie?"

"It's Meghan," Meghan said softly as her eyes widened. "My name is Meghan."

"Whatever," Paula responded. "Melanie, Meghan, it's all the same. But seriously, I want dessert now. Can you take my order?"

Meghan was shocked by Paula's rudeness, but she dutifully nodded. "Sure. Can I bring you some tarts? That's the dessert special tonight."

Paula rolled her eyes. "Ugh, what a boring dessert," she announced. "Just bring me some ice cream."

"No problem," Meghan said as she nodded at Kirsty and Paula. Meghan's heart pounded with frustration as she walked away from the head table. Paula had been *nasty*, and Meghan was disappointed that someone she had been so excited to meet had turned out to be so unfriendly.

"Melanie?"

Meghan turned around to find a bespectacled man waving her down. "It's Meghan," she said to the man.

"My apologies, and apologies on behalf of Mrs. Brown," the man said. "I'm her personal assistant. She is a little fussy today, but I promise, she is usually a doll."

Meghan shrugged. "I'm sure," she answered. "Can I help you with something?"

The man nodded. "Yes, actually; Mrs. Brown wanted me to tell you that she wants dairy-free, vegan, sugar-free ice cream."

Meghan gritted her teeth. "Of course she does," she muttered under her breath. "I'll be back with that in a moment."

The personal assistant scurried away, and Meghan took three long deep breaths to calm herself down. "This is the Governor's Ball," she told herself as she walked along the perimeter of the dance floor in search of ice cream for Paula. "I need to enjoy the night and not let her get to me. After I fetch the ice cream, I'll find Jack, and we'll dance the night away."

Just as Meghan thought of her boyfriend, she spotted him across the room. He looked more handsome than ever in his tuxedo, and Meghan admired the way it hugged his muscled shoulders. She smiled, feeling a warmth in her heart that spread to her cheeks, putting a bright red blush on her face. Meghan turned toward Jack, eager to surprise him, but before she could reach him, a stunningly beautiful auburn-haired woman leaned in to kiss him on the cheek. Jack laughed, and Meghan's heart dropped as he embraced the woman.

"Who could that be?" Meghan asked herself as her hands clenched into fists.

Just as Meghan neared her boyfriend, a shrill scream filled the room. All heads turned, and in the middle of the dance floor, a woman was lying on the floor.

"Help! Help! Help!"

Meghan recognized Kirsty's voice; Kirsty sounded panicked, and Meghan rushed to her side. Kirsty was hunched down and leaning over Paula Brown. Paula's eyes were rolled back in her head, and her face was ashen. Kirsty tapped on Paula's chest repeatedly, crying and shouting as Meghan took her by the shoulders.

"What is going on?" Meghan asked as she stared into Kirsty's worried face. A crowd formed around the women, and Meghan heard whispers as she looked down at Paula's still body.

"We were walking over to meet the Governor, and before I knew it, she had collapsed."

"What's going on here?"

Meghan and Kirsty saw Jack run to them, taking off his tuxedo Jacket and leaning over Paula's body. "Kirsty, Meghan, I need the two of you to back away."

"Do you need help, Jack?" Chief Nunan asked as she walked through the crowd.

Jack shook his head. "Chief," he said slowly. "She's dead. Call for the coroner, Chief Nunan. Paula Brown has fallen down dead."

5

The morning after the Governor's Ball, Meghan felt a dull ache in her heart as she walked her dogs along the shoreline; she had been so excited to experience the grandeur of the ball, and everything had been ruined by Paula Brown's unexpected death in the early hours of the event. As Meghan tugged her little dogs along the pebbly beach, she could not shake the melancholy threatening to send tears spilling down her cheeks.

"Meghan?"

She nearly jumped out of her skin as Claude walked up behind her. Without his fancy chef hat, he was nearly unrecognizable in his street clothes, and the dark, heavy bags underneath his eyes suggested that he had not slept well.

"Claude," she said softly.

"What a small world," Claude replied as he raised an eyebrow at her. This is a lonely little place to be, all alone, so early in the morning."

Meghan pointed at the Pacific Ocean. "The waves always calm me," she told him as the dark blue water crashed along the beach. "After last night, I needed some peace."

Claude stared into Meghan's eyes. "The ball was never going to go on again after last night," he declared as Meghan looked down at her feet. "The Governor's Ball is forever ruined, marked by the death of Paula Brown."

Meghan shook her head. "It is so sad," she said. "Such a tragedy."

"Indeed, it was," he agreed. "So unexpected for her to pass away. It is strange, though, Meghan. I have heard that she had only been at the event for a short time, and knowing Paula personally, I know that she does not eat on days she attends events. The only food she would have had at the ball would have been the Welcome Tarts set out at the head table. The tarts that *you* happened to make…"

Meghan's body grew cold as she processed Claude's words. "What exactly are you trying to say to me?" she asked as Fiesta and Siesta skipped through the water.

Claude sighed. "I'm not saying *anything*, Meghan Truman," he haughtily replied. "But I can say that your treats had been served to Paula, and she had taken a bite of her tart. Kirsty Fisher told me that. And I can also tell you that that fact alone makes you look very, very interesting to the police, Meghan."

Meghan shook her head. "I didn't make the tarts," she argued. "My team arrived at the event hours before I did; they used my recipe, but I didn't personally make the tarts, Claude. And who is to say that the tarts had anything to do with her death?"

Claude bit his lip. "I'm not saying that. But, I did check on your team in the kitchen early in the day, and that assistant of yours? Trudy? Well, she should be called Broody Trudy; her attitude was terrible, and she lacked professionalism. Meghan. I'm just saying, if Broody Trudy had gotten angry and wanted to frame you, or wanted to do away with Paula for the fun of it, it wouldn't surprise me."

"That is *enough.*"

Jack Irvin walked up to Claude and Meghan, his own dog, Dash, barking happily at Fiesta and Siesta. "Claude, that is enough; the Sandy Bay Police Department is investigating Paula's death, and it is inappropriate of you to say such things to Meghan."

Meghan raised an eyebrow at Jack. "Hey, Jack," she said coolly. "Nice to see you here today."

Claude looked between Meghan and Jack. "I sense some trouble in paradise with you two lovebirds," he declared in his thick accent.

Jack cocked his head to the side. "Trouble?"

Claude winked at Jack. "I would be in trouble too if I had been paying attention to gorgeous auburn-haired ladies instead of my own date."

Jack's jaw dropped. "Meghan? What is he talking about?"

Meghan crossed her arms across her chest and said nothing. Claude grinned antagonistically. "She didn't say anything, but I saw this lady's date chatting with someone else last night just before Paula dropped dead. Perhaps you two have some talking to do."

Jack frowned. "Meghan, I *was* talking to another woman, but you should have come over to say hello. It was Michelle. We were catching up, and she wanted to meet you."

Meghan glared at Jack. "After I saw her kiss your cheek, I didn't think that I should interrupt your conversation," she pouted.

Jack gasped. "Meghan," he said in shock. "I told you that Michelle is one of my old friends. There's nothing between us. She gave me a friendly peck. It was nothing."

"For it being nothing, someone sounds rather defensive," Claude sneered as Meghan crossed her arms across her chest.

"Look, man," Jack said as he turned to address Claude.

"This is between *us*. Besides, you were summoned down to the police station for some initial questioning; if you say one more word, I'll take you down there in handcuffs."

Claude waved a hand dismissively. "Please," he muttered. "You Americans…"

Jack puffed up his chest. "What did you say to me? Say it to my face."

Meghan stepped between the two men, nearly choking on the thick, musky scent of Claude's cologne. "Stop it," Meghan ordered as she placed a hand on Jack's chest and tried to shoo Claude away. "This is ridiculous. Claude, the police will get to the bottom of Paula's death. Stop asking me questions and making matters worse. Jack, you and I need to have a private conversation. Why don't you just go on home, and we can talk later."

Claude turned on his expensive heeled leather shoes and stormed away. Jack looked sadly at Meghan.

"Meghan…"

Meghan put a finger to his lips. "Shhhh," she demanded. "Don't talk to me right now. My night and my dreams for the evening were destroyed, and you didn't make anything better. Right now, I wouldn't mind if I never had to look at you again, Jack Irvin."

6

_____

That evening, Meghan was desperate to get out of her terrible mood. She had tried all of her usual tricks; from taking a long bubble bath, to a cozy cup of jasmine tea, to indulging in chocolate covered cherries, her favorite candy, nothing was helping to settle her spirits. She was annoyed by Claude's not-so-veiled suggestion that _she_ had had something to do with Paula Brown's death. She was upset that Jack had been too preoccupied with catching up with Michelle to be by her side at the ball, and she was devastated that the event had ended not with her business gaining even more attention, but that someone had perished without warning and the Governor's Ball was now considered a tragedy.

As Meghan lay beneath her goose feather comforter, she breathed in deeply as the sound of the rain pulled her into a state of relaxation. It was a dreary evening; the air was bitterly cold, and the rain pounded upon the roof of Meghan's apartment. "I have to pull myself out of this funk," she murmured to herself as Fiesta licked her ankle. "I've wasted too much time today being grumpy; last night was not what I expected, but I need to pull it together. I know what I will do. I will march myself downstairs and work on a new recipe. I've been dreaming of experimenting with straw-berry extract and fresh basil for a batch of scones, and what better time to try something new."

Ten minutes later, Meghan was happily kneading dough and singing to herself as she dreamed of a delicious new way to bake her famous scones. As she cut the tops off of the enormous, juicy red strawberries she had specially purchased from an organic farm in Mexico, she heard a knock at the door.

"Who could that be?" she wondered aloud as she walked to the yellow door and peered out of the peephole. A short, plump man looked up at her, and she opened the door. "Can I help you? We're closed tonight."

The man shrugged. "It's cold and rainy," he said, adjusting the collar of his tan trench coat. "Any chance you could spare a cup of coffee for a drenched stranger?"

Meghan saw that the man was covered in rain. Her heart sank as she thought of turning him away, and she stepped back to gesture him inside. "Come on in," she warmly invited the man. "I don't have any fresh coffee, but I do have some jasmine tea, my favorite."

"Perfect," the man breathed as he took a seat at one of the little white iron tables in the dining area. "I've been trying to find something that's open all night, and this town is *dead*."

"I'm not surprised," Meghan admitted as she delivered the steaming cup of tea to the man. "With what happened at the Governor's Ball that night, a lot of people in town have closed down their businesses for the next few days."

The man leaned in, raising an eyebrow and placing his hand on his chin as he listened intently. "Can you tell me more about what happened? I'm not really from here…"

Meghan sat down at the table across from the man.

"Don't mind if I ramble," Meghan said as she leaned back in her seat. "It's been a tough twenty-four hours, and if you don't mind, I would love to just vent."

The man smiled. "Go on. I'm here to listen."

Meghan tucked her dark hair behind her ears and continued. "It all started when I was asked to make the desserts for the event. Then I found out that my stupid boyfriend, Jack, had gotten tickets to the ball from…"

* * *

"I'm glad we could do this," Jack said cautiously as Meghan sipped her caramel latte. "I know this is your favorite coffee shop, and I thought a cozy little coffee date would be the perfect place to talk things through."

It was the morning after Meghan had opened the bakery to the stranger, and after a pleading voicemail from Jack, along with a barrage of text messages and emails, Meghan had agreed to meet with him in person to discuss the Governor's Ball.

"It was really nothing, Meghan," he assured her as she crossed her left leg over her right leg and stiffened in her seat. "Michelle is just an old pal. You have to believe me."

Meghan shook her head. "It just looked like an awfully familiar moment between the pair of you," she informed her boyfriend as he sat nervously across from her. "The kiss she gave you…I didn't like it, Jack."

Jack buried his head in his hands, and Meghan saw his shoulders begin to shake. "I'm so sorry, Meghan," he whimpered. "I should have introduced the two of you before the event. I should have stayed by your side and followed closely behind when Claude whisked you away. This is all my fault."

Meghan felt the warm rush of relief; Jack knew that he

had made a mistake, and he was admitting to his poor decision-making, as well as providing a satisfactory apology. Meghan could see that he was upset, and she wanted nothing more than to wrap her arms around Jack and comfort him.

"Hey, Meghan? Saw you in the paper this morning. Have you seen this?"

Meghan shook her head as Stanley, the owner of her favorite coffee shop, slapped a newspaper on the table in front of her. "Check this out, Meghan," Stanley said with a stern look in his eye.

Jack snatched the paper from Meghan and began to read the article. "Sitting in her bakery, all alone on a cold, dreary night, Meghan Truman should have been comforted by her boyfriend, local detective Jack Irvin," Jack read aloud.

"What is this?" Meghan asked. "What on Earth? Is this a satire?"

Jack continued, "Meghan Truman had a lot to say about the night of the Governor's Ball. She had a lot to say about Paula Brown, the former Miss Texas and now late wife to our beloved Governor. She had a lot to say about her bakery, and her hopes and dreams for Truly Sweet, a treasured establishment in downtown Sandy Bay. Meghan Truman also had a lot to say about her boyfriend, and his lack of good judgement on the night of the ball."

Meghan stared at Jack, her dark eyes wide as his face turned red. "Jack? I have no idea where this came from…."

Meghan reached over and grabbed the newspaper from Jack. She glanced down at the author's name, and when she saw the author's tiny headshot in the corner of the page, she shrieked. "That was the man in the bakery last night!"

Jack stood up. "What man? Are you serious, Meghan? You got angry that I said hello to an old friend, and then you blabbed about me to some guy at your bakery?"

Meghan shook her head. "I didn't know he was a

reporter," she protested as Jack turned to walk toward the door. "I thought he was a customer at Truly Sweet."

Jack stopped. "You talk about me like this to customers?" he asked as Meghan's eyes filled with tears.

"No, Jack, please understand. It was a long day, and this stranger wandered into the bakery. I didn't know he was a reporter. I started chatting with him, and after everything that happened, I just lost it and began to vent. I don't talk about you to other people, I promise."

Jack scoffed. "It sure looks like you did some damage with this article, Meghan. I am humiliated. I am leaving. We can talk about this later."

Meghan tugged on Jack's sleeve. "Jack, *please*," she begged as Jack walked to the door. "Don't leave like this; I didn't mean what I said about you. I was just angry."

Jack frowned. "I'm still humiliated. I don't want to talk about this any further in public, Meghan. I'll call you tomorrow, or maybe the next day, and we can settle things then."

Meghan began to sob as Jack left the coffee shop. Stanley, who had been watching the encounter from his station at the register, came to Meghan's side. "Meghan?"

Meghan sniffled. "Yeah, Stanley?"

Stanley grimaced. "That was a scene, Meghan, and I can't have a scene in my establishment. You're going to need to go."

Meghan's jaw dropped. "You're kicking me out?"

Stanley nodded. "Sorry, but this is a no-drama zone, Meghan. That looked like a lot of drama to me."

Meghan gathered her red purse and her latte and walked outside. She shivered as the freezing air hit her skin, and she balled her hands into fists thinking of the life she left behind in Los Angeles to move to Sandy Bay. "Los Angeles was a no-drama zone," Meghan muttered as she walked home. "I moved to this town hoping for a fresh start, expecting a small town to be sweet and pleasant, not filled with unexpected deaths, murders, and *my* reputation constantly on the line. I'm sick of all of this! If something doesn't change, I am of half a mind to pack up my things and leave Sandy Bay *for good.*"

7

"The sun is unusually bright today," Jacqueline complained as she adjusted her sunglasses across her ski-slope nose. "It's winter in the Pacific Northwest, and the sun is practically blinding me."

Meghan adjusted the green woolen scarf she had wound around her neck. "I'm not complaining," she told Jackie as the two women stood together in Sandy Bay Square. "It's warmer than it usually is, and if we are going to stand outside in the winter all afternoon, I would much rather the day be too sunny than too chilly."

Meghan and Jacqueline stood amongst hundreds of Sandy Bay residents for a special ceremony that had been hastily scheduled to memorialize Paula Brown. The governor himself had traveled back to Sandy Bay to dedicate a plaque in the square in honor of his late wife, and the entire town had gathered for the ceremony.

"You know, it *is* bright out here," Meghan admitted as she shielded her eyes from the bright sunshine. "It feels a little wrong to have such a somber ceremony on a beautiful day."

"I can't believe Governor Brown is out and about so soon

after his wife passed away," Jacqueline whispered into Meghan's ear as Kirsty Fisher approached the platform that had been set up in the middle of the square.

"Attention, everyone," Kirsty called out in a quivering voice as she ascended the platform and stepped forward to speak into the microphone. "Good afternoon. My name is Kirsty Fisher, and I was one of Paula's closest friends."

Meghan raised an eyebrow at Jacqueline. "Were they really?"

Jacqueline shook her head. "Maybe in Kirsty's mind...you know how she likes to put on airs!"

Meghan giggled, but then silenced herself upon seeing the stern look from the couple standing next to her.

"The tragedy of Paula's death is unforgettable, but we have gathered here today to commemorate her passing with something special. The Governor has brought a special plaque to dedicate to Paula's memory. I thank you all for being here today, and I hope that we can all send our thoughts and good wishes to the governor at this time."

The Governor appeared behind Kirsty, and she kissed him on both cheeks. Meghan noticed that he looked exhausted; with dark, deep bags beneath his eyes, and red, swollen eyes, Meghan's heart ached for the governor, despite his wife's rudeness toward her at the ball.

"Thank you, Kristy," Governor Brown said as Kirsty wiped a tear from her eye with a monogrammed handkerchief.

"See?" Jackie muttered. "If his wife and *Kirsty* were truly dear friends, surely the governor would know her name...."

"Shhhhhh," Meghan hushed as the Governor continued.

"Paula had a vibrant, exciting life; she was Miss Texas, she was a film star, and most recently, she was my beloved wife and the first-lady of our state...."

"Excuse me? Meghan Truman?"

Meghan jumped as someone tapped her shoulder. She turned around and squinted; the sun was directly in her eyes, and she could hardly make out the figure in front of her. Meghan could tell it was a woman, and she held a hand in front of her face to shield it from the bright light.

"I'm with the Governor's staff," the woman explained quietly. "He would like to speak with you after the event. Take this pass and go to the VIP tent after his talk."

Meghan blinked in confusion, calling out as the woman turned and walked away, "Why does the Governor want to talk to me?"

The woman did not answer, and Meghan turned to Jacqueline. "What was that all about?"

Jacqueline shook her head. "I have no idea," she replied. "That woman was gorgeous. I wonder what she does on the Governor's staff."

Twenty minutes later, the Governor finished his speech, and Meghan took off toward the VIP tent. She pushed through the crowd, careful as she wove through the people politely clapping for the Governor. When she reached the tent, a uniformed guard examined her pass, and then he waved her inside.

"Ahhh, Meghan Truman."

Meghan's hand flew to her mouth in shock as the Governor greeted her by name.

"Thank you for joining us here, Meghan," the Governor said graciously as he loosened his blue checkered tie and took a seat on a white folding chair. "Please, sit."

Meghan sat down on a black folding chair, and the Governor took her hand in his. "My assistants and Paula's assistants informed me that she was a bit…brisk to you at the event. My apologies, Meghan."

Meghan cocked her head to the side as she glanced around the tent. A table filled with deli meats and cheeses was on the far right side, and generators were plugged in to warm the small space.

"How do you know who I am?" Meghan asked.

The Governor chuckled. "It was my ball, remember? The ball is my favorite event each year, and I make it my business to know who is coming and going. I've actually been enjoying your desserts for months now; my assistants have an order sent over each week, and it was my idea to feature your treats at the event."

Meghan blushed. "That explains the order we send to the capital each week," she murmured. "Thank you for thinking of me. Your business means a lot to me. I'm also so sorry about your wife. She was a hero of mine when I was a child. I'm from Texas originally, and I always admired her spirit."

The Governor took Meghan's hand and gave it a squeeze. "Thank you for saying that," he said softly. "It was a shock when my wife died—the police are suggesting it was a murder, can you believe that? I am devastated, but I am so glad I got to come to Sandy Bay today to lay the plaque."

Before Meghan could respond, a young man came to the Governor's side and whispered in his ear. "Oh, excuse me, Meghan," the Governor apologized. "My assistant here says I have a conference call scheduled. I will be right back!"

As the Governor left the tent, Meghan was shocked when Jack walked inside. "Jack?" Meghan asked. "What are you doing here?"

Jack nodded at the walkie-talkie in his hand. "You would know if you would answer my calls," he muttered. "I'm working security. I saw you come in here, and I wanted to make sure you are okay. What were you and the Governor discussing?"

Meghan tossed her dark hair behind her shoulder. "That's really not your business," she said. "Your *friend*, Michelle, is on his staff. Why don't you go ask her?"

Jack narrowed his eyes at Meghan. "Don't talk like that, Meghan," he said. "Michelle is here today, but she is just a friend. In fact, she was the one who gave you the pass to come back here."

Meghan gasped. "I didn't recognize her," she replied. "The sun was so bright, and I didn't know it was your friend from the dance floor."

Jack crossed his arms across his chest. "Meghan," he began. "We have to talk about this. Michelle is just a friend, and if you can't accept that... well, I'm afraid that if you cannot get over this Michelle thing, we are really going to need to have a serious conversation about our future as a couple. I can't do this for much longer, Meghan, and if we need to break up, then let's just do it now."

8

As Meghan sipped her caramel latte, her heart sank as she recounted the chaos of her evening; following her quarrel with Jack, the couple had met in the park to discuss their relationship. After two hours of fighting, Meghan and Jack had decided to remain a couple, but both parties knew that they needed some time apart. They decided to take a few days away from each other, and while Meghan was sad that she and Jack were going through a rough patch, she was happy that they had decided to stay together as a couple.

The other chaotic part of Meghan's evening took place upon Meghan's return from her lengthy conversation with Jack. As Meghan walked into the bakery, she heard Trudy screaming at Pamela from across the dining room.

"I don't care if you are talented, or pretty, or the Queen of England," Trudy snarled as Pamela cried. "I am Meghan's assistant, and when she is gone, I am in charge!"

Meghan saw Pamela's lip quiver. "I only asked if I could help with a different project, Trudy. I didn't mean to make you mad."

Before Trudy could speak, Meghan held her hands up. "What is going on in here? Trudy? What is the meaning of this?"

Trudy shook her head. "That little girl just prances around here like she owns the place."

Meghan frowned. "Pamela is a great help to us, Trudy," she argued. "And as the owner of this place, Trudy, I have concerns we need to address. Pamela? If you could take your things and head home for the night, I think Trudy and I really need to speak in private."

Pamela nodded, and she gathered her jacket and back-pack. "Bye, Meghan. Bye, Trudy."

Once Pamela had closed the door, Meghan sat down at one of the little white tables. She gestured for Trudy to join her.

"I have some concerns, Trudy," Meghan informed her employee as Trudy glared at her. "Your attitude has been concerning. Can you please help me understand what is going on? You've seemed tense here, and I even received some complaints about your professionalism at the ball. I heard you were snippy with some of the guests, and I also heard that you had a camera out and were taking selfies. You know we cannot do that at an event. That is unacceptable."

Trudy's jaw dropped. "Are you serious? People are talking about me? What the heck, Meghan? I can't believe this. All I do is work my tail off here, and you make me feel bad by saying these things?"

Meghan shook her head. "No, Trudy," she protested, placing a hand on Trudy's shoulder. "I am worried about you. You have always been happy-go-lucky, and lately, it's seemed as if something is wrong."

Trudy rose from the table. As she turned to leave, she stopped and waved a fist at Meghan. "This is ridiculous. See if I don't go join some other bakery, Meghan. I am sick of the games and nonsense."

Trudy stormed out of Truly Sweet, and Meghan forced herself to take three long, slow breaths. "Well, that was *exactly* what I wanted to deal with after a long argument with Jack," Meghan muttered sarcastically. "Ugh, I need to take a walk and clear my head."

Meghan gathered her red purse and locked up the bakery. She was happy that the air wasn't too cold, and she tucked her hair behind her ears as she wandered through the town.

"Two wrongs don't make a right," Meghan thought to herself as she walked. "And I want Trudy to be back to her normal, cheerful self. I know what I will do! I will go down to the fruit market and get a basket for her; maybe if Trudy knows how much I appreciate her, she will relax a bit. I will get the basket for her and surprise her with all of her favorites, and maybe things will go back to normal."

Meghan smiled to herself as she imagined the happy look on Trudy's face when she surprised her with the fruit basket. She set off toward the fruit market, eager to make things right with her assistant. As Meghan perused the aisles of fresh fruit, she noticed a familiar-looking man staring at her from across the market. "That's odd," Meghan thought as she studied the man's face. "Where have I seen him before?"

Suddenly, Meghan remembered why she recognized him; the man was Paula Brown's personal assistant. They had spoken briefly at the Governor's Ball. Knowing that the man was probably mourning his late employer, Meghan decided she needed to give her condolences. She put the fruit back in its bin and made her way over to the man.

"Hey," Meghan said softly. "Do you remember me? I'm Meghan. You are Paula Brown's assistant, yes?"

The man looked down at his shoes. "I *was* her assistant," he gently corrected. "Rest in peace, poor Paula."

Meghan touched his arm. "I'm so sorry for your loss. Paula must have been such an interesting woman to work for. What was your name?"

"I'm Donnie," the man said. "Meghan, I'm glad you said hello."

Meghan nodded. "Of course," she said. "How are you doing? What a difficult time it must be for you."

Donnie shrugged. "It hasn't been easy," he admitted. "But Governor Brown is a good guy; he's offered to find me another spot within his own staff, and I am so thankful to be employed by the Browns."

Meghan smiled. "He seemed like a kind man."

Donnie agreed. "He is the best," Donnie told Meghan. "I have learned so much from the Browns. I want to get into politics myself someday, and I am in such a better position now that I've had so much exposure to the way they do things. It isn't easy; the Governor demands excellence, as did Paula, but I can only thank them for the experiences I've gained."

Meghan placed a hand on her heart. "That is a wonderful thing to say about your employer," she gushed. "I can only hope my employees feel that way about me."

Donnie smiled. "I'm sure they do. You seem like a nice gal. Anyway, I need to run, but I have to tell you that your treats were fantastic. I loved your tarts at the event, and I've been craving more."

Meghan reached into her purse and fetched a Truly Sweet gift card. "Here," she said as she pressed the card into Donnie's hands. "Take this. Swing by any time for a treat; it's *my* treat!"

Donnie grinned. "You are adorable. I will have to talk to the Governor to see if we can do a mass order of your treats for his mansion and offices. I know you already do a shipment to him each week, but I think a mass order would be better for all involved."

She clapped her hands in excitement. "You would do that for me? You just met me, Donnie."

He winked at Meghan. "You seem truly sweet, Meghan," he cooed. "What kind of future politician would I be if I didn't extend a hand out to the little people every once in a while?"

9

"That looks so good on you, Meghan!" Jacqueline gushed as Meghan showed off a chunky knit sweater. "Olive is definitely your color; it makes your skin just *glow*! That would make for such a cute outfit for New Year's Eve."

Meghan spun around in the dressing room of Smitten Kitten, the women's boutique around the corner from Truly Sweet. Jackie had suggested a little shopping date to get Meghan's mind off of Jack, and Meghan had gladly taken her up on the invitation.

"Are you sure it isn't too flashy?" Meghan asked as she stared at the sweater's square neckline. "These puffy sleeves feel a little too high fashion for plain old me."

Jacqueline smacked Meghan playfully on the bottom. "Meghan, you are beautiful. Your thick, dark hair is the envy of every girl in Sandy Bay, your dark eyes have that sparkle to them, and your smile brightens every room you walk into. That sweater fits your body perfectly, Meghan, and I would be a bad friend if I didn't let you buy it. Besides, it's winter now. Surely you need a few cute new pieces for your wardrobe. This isn't warm Los Angeles, after all."

Meghan glanced back at herself in the mirror. "I think you're right," she admitted to Jacqueline. "This is a good color for me, and I do like the way this sweater fits. Okay, Jackie, you have convinced me. Add it to my pile."

"Yes!" Jacqueline said. "Hey, Meghan? Now that it's been a few days… well, I hate to ask, but what happened at the ball? I didn't want to ask too many questions, but since you seem so relaxed… and it's just us two in this dressing room. Care to share?"

Meghan sighed. "It's fine," she relented. "At the ball, Paula was a bit rude to me, and I was upset. I went looking for Jack, and I saw him getting a kiss on the cheek from some stupid girl he was friends with back in the day."

"I wondered why the pair of you were taking a few days off," Jacqueline said as she handed another sweater to Meghan to try on. "Who is the girl?"

Meghan rolled her eyes. "Jack says she is just a friend, but from the looks of it, it seemed a bit fishy; she was one of those drop dead gorgeous girls who just looks like she could sneakily steal a boyfriend from right underneath someone's nose."

Jacqueline shook her head. "That's awful," she said. "I can't believe Jack would talk to someone like that."

Meghan laughed sadly. "You know how guys are when they see a pretty face."

Jackie watched as Meghan slipped a soft blue turtleneck over her head. "No," Jackie dismissed as she looked at Meghan's torso. "That isn't flattering. Take it off."

Meghan obeyed, removing the sweater and hanging it on the rack in the dressing room. "I think I have enough new clothes to last me a lifetime," Meghan told Jacqueline as she giggled at the pile of skirts, tops, underthings, and accessories. "Let's get out of here, Jackie; I don't think my bank account can take any more major hits!"

Jacqueline chuckled, and the two women gathered around the pile of clothes. As they exited the dressing room, they ran straight into a thin, auburn-haired woman who was sitting primly in a love seat in the corner of the main dressing area. It was Michelle, Jack's friend. Meghan gasped.

"Meghan," Michelle said coolly, her hands clenched together and resting on her left knee. "Pleasure seeing you here. I can't say it was a pleasure *hearing* you, though; do you often speak ill of people behind their backs in public?"

Before Meghan could respond, Jacqueline stepped forward. "She doesn't speak ill of people who aren't trying to steal her boyfriend!"

Michelle laughed. "I'm not trying to steal anyone's boyfriend," she informed Meghan and Jackie as she flashed her left hand at the women and dangled her ring finger in front of her face. "I'm engaged, ladies."

Meghan stared at the enormous, princess-cut diamond ring glittering on Michelle's hand, but Jacqueline continued, "why would an engaged woman buy a ticket that expensive for Meghan's boyfriend to go to the ball? That doesn't make sense, Michelle."

Michelle rolled her eyes. "You two are acting like children; those tickets were free for us working for the Governor, and after chatting with Jack and hearing him rave about his girlfriend, the famous Meghan Truman, I thought it would be a *kind* gesture to offer him a free ticket. Had I known that Jack's girlfriend would speak so poorly of me, in public, nonetheless, perhaps I would have given that ticket to my own fiance."

Meghan's body grew hot with shame. "I'm sorry," she whispered to Michelle. "I spoke too soon; it was so kind of you to get the ticket for Jack, and I shouldn't have judged you before I met you. That wasn't fair."

Michelle rose from the love seat and shook her head. "Too little, too late, Meghan," she hissed to her. "You cross me once, and you don't get the chance to cross me again."

Jackie raised an eyebrow. "What is that supposed to mean?"

Michelle smirked. "I'll be something big someday," she informed Meghan and Jackie. "Just you wait; the Governor is grooming me to take over his role someday, and sooner than later, little twerps like you two will mean nothing to me. I'll be in charge, and you two will still be pathetic little nobodies in this pathetic little town."

As Meghan stared, Michelle collected her purse and tossed her auburn hair behind her narrow shoulders. She sashayed out of the dressing area, and Meghan's eye filled with tears. "She heard me being so mean and petty," she cried as Jackie shook her head. "Michelle *hates* me, Trudy is still angry at me, and Jack and I haven't spoken in two days. What else could go wrong, Jackie?"

10

The next morning, Meghan was trying to hide her low spirits from Pamela as the two iced cupcakes at the bakery. Despite leaving the fruit basket at Trudy's door several days earlier, Trudy was not returning Meghan's calls, and Meghan was concerned that her relationship with her assistant was ruined. As the day went on, Meghan continued to fret, and finally, she decided it was time to call it a day.

"Pamela? I know it's early, but I'm going to close up shop; you can clock out at your scheduled time, but why don't you finish up those cupcakes and then get out of here?"

Pamela nodded. "Sure thing, Meghan. I'll wrap these up and then see you tomorrow."

Meghan began to clean the kitchen, and as she scrubbed the dough stuck between the metal ridges of her mixing spoons, she ventured deeper and deeper into her own thoughts. She barely registered the sound of Pamela leaving, and as Meghan tidied the kitchen, she pondered her predicaments.

"Maybe I could send an apology note over to Michelle,"

Meghan thought as she poured soap into a wooden bowl. "I wasn't happy about her connection with Jack, but it sounds like I was the one who jumped the gun. I feel terrible that she overheard us."

Meghan pulled out a tiny bristle brush and began to scrub a set of knives. "And Trudy…if she doesn't answer my calls soon, I am just going to have to go over to her house. She has been a dear friend and a valuable employee. I can't lose her."

Meghan bit her bottom lip as she thought of her greatest worry, the issue that had been tugging at her heartstrings. "And Jack… what am I going to do about Jack? I was so angry at him, but it sounds like I may have been out of line…"

Suddenly, Meghan felt a tap on her shoulder. She reached for one of the knives, gripping it sharply in her left hand and slowly turning to face whoever was behind her. Meghan quickly held up the knife in front of her face, waving it back and forth and screaming.

"Meghan, stop screaming, it's just *me!*"

Meghan was stunned to find Jack standing before her, his blue eyes red and his blonde hair messy. She placed a hand on her racing heart and lowered the knife. "What are you doing here, Jack?"

Jack gestured toward the door. "Didn't you hear me come in? I walked right inside and shouted your name."

Meghan shook her head. "I was day-dreaming," she admitted as adrenaline filled her body. "I had no idea you were here."

Jack sighed. "Meghan, we need to talk…"

Meghan nodded emphatically. "Yes, we do. Can we sit in the dining room?"

Meghan and Jack walked into the dining room and sat across from each other at one of the little white tables. "I want to say I'm sorry," Jack began as he folded his hands atop the table. "I should have been more considerate of your feelings, Meghan. Michelle is honestly just a friend; she has a fiancé of her own who she is very much in love with, but I should have explained more to you before throwing her into the mix. I've been trying to get close to her so that maybe someday, I could get a job with the Governor."

Meghan nodded. "Jack, thank you so much for apologizing," she said to him as she reached over to take his hands in hers. "But I was the one who jumped to conclusions. I let my emotions get the best of me, and I should have taken a moment to truly listen to you and what you were telling me. I want to apologize to you, Jack. I am sorry I was nasty, I am sorry I didn't take you at your word, and I am sorry that we didn't have this conversation sooner. That day we met to talk in the park was so difficult; I was exhausted and so confused, and I wish we had been able to talk like *this*."

Jack rose from the table. He pulled Meghan up with him and gathered her in his arms. Jack wrapped his arms around Meghan's waist, moving her closer to him until she could feel the beating of his heart. "Meghan," Jack whispered in Meghan's ear. "Meghan, I *love* you. We have been through so much together since you moved to Sandy Bay, and I don't want to lose you."

Meghan blushed, the heat rising to her cheeks as she placed her hands on Jack's face. "You love me? You've never told me that before."

Jack nodded. "I thought about it this whole week," he told her as he stared into her dark eyes. "I missed you, Meghan. Even agreeing to take a few days away from you felt... wrong. You are right for me, and I love you."

Jack kissed Meghan gently on the lips, running a hand through her dark hair as she leaned into his embrace. "I love you too, Jack," she murmured.

Jack grinned as he pulled away. "I was hoping you would say that," he admitted. "I am so happy to hear that."

Meghan beamed. "Well, can we celebrate being fully back together and being in love? I have some carrot cake in the back that I know you will love..."

Jack shook his head, and Meghan could see the disappointment in his eyes. "I hate to say it, but I'm actually here on official business."

Meghan raised an eyebrow. "What do you mean?"

Jack shrugged. "There have been some new developments in the investigation of Paula's death. It has officially been ruled a murder, and our lab reports indicate that she died from overdosing on some small tablets. We believe the tablets were slipped into something she ate at the event, and we are talking with every single person who was in the kitchen last night."

Meghan gasped. "But I wasn't in the kitchen! I was a guest. You know that."

Jack agreed. "I do know that, but unfortunately, Trudy and Pamela were not guests. I have been ordered to follow up with everyone, and I was hoping to find them both here."

Meghan sighed. "Pamela is probably at home," she told Jack. "But Trudy...I don't know where Trudy is. She's been acting so out of sorts lately, Jack."

Jack furrowed his brow. "Do you think she had anything to do with Paula's murder?"

Meghan's jaw dropped. "Jack... she's been acting so odd. What if she did? She had access to the ice cream, and I know she takes a variety of medicines for her back. What if Trudy slipped some pills into the ice cream and killed Paula?"

Jack frowned. "It sounds like I need to speak with her immediately, Meghan. I'll send a deputy out to her house to collect her, as well as Pamela."

Meghan nodded. "I'm coming with you," she said. "They are my employees, and if anything happens, I want to be there. I doubt that Pamela had anything to do with Paula's death, but the more we talk about it, the more I think that Trudy knows something."

Jack reached for his coat and fastened the buttons. "Well, I'll call the deputy right now."

Meghan shook her head. "No," she told Jack. "I'll go to Trudy's house. Truly Sweet's reputation would be ruined if she was the one who poisoned Paula, and I want to talk to her *myself.*"

eghan walked quickly up the stone path to Trudy's house. She had never been to Trudy's house before, and she was in awe of the tall, majestic evergreen trees that lined the walkway to Trudy's front door. "I hope this goes well," Meghan thought to herself as she knocked on the front door. "If Trudy had anything to do with Paula's death, I will be *devastated*."

Trudy answered the door after two knocks. "What do you want?" Trudy asked Meghan, her eyes narrowed.

Meghan took a deep breath. "Trudy, you've been acting so strange lately, and I just wanted to check on you. The police have some questions to ask you, and instead of sending a squad car for you, I volunteered to take you to the station. I want to talk with you. I care about you, Trudy, and if you're mixed up in some bad news, I want to help."

Trudy sighed. "Let's go for a walk, shall we?"

Meghan nodded, pleased that Trudy had not slammed the door in her face. The two women took off toward town. Trudy's eyes were cast down at her shoes, and Meghan gently put a hand on Trudy's shoulder. "Trudy, what's wrong?"

Trudy turned away from Meghan. "It's nothing," Trudy griped at Meghan. "I just get sick of you siding with Pamela over me. You're always taking her side, and I'm just left by myself."

Hearing the hurt in Trudy's voice, Meghan tried again. "Trudy," she murmured. "What's going on with you? You haven't been yourself for a while, and I am concerned."

Trudy began to cry. "I'm sorry," she sputtered as she wiped a tear from her cheek. "You're right. I haven't been myself. It's the anniversary month of my son's passing; he died ten years ago this month, and this time of year is always hard for me."

Meghan reached for Trudy and gathered her in her arms. "Oh, Trudy," Meghan said as she hugged her assistant. "I am so sorry for your loss. I had no idea."

Trudy wiped her nose on her sleeve. "It's fine," she said softly. "I don't tell a lot of people; I don't want to be a burden."

Meghan shook her head. "Trudy," she said. "You're my friend. Your sadness is something I want to know about so I can help."

"Thanks, Meghan," she whispered. "It's just been a difficult month. I'm sorry I've had an attitude. I'm sorry I was rude and taking selfies at the event; my grandson, the son of my late son, got a new phone with a really good camera for me during Thanksgiving, and taking photos has been the only thing taking my mind off of my late son. My grandson asked me to take some photos at the ball; he *adored* Paula Brown's old movies, and he wanted to see if I could snap some pictures of her. I actually have it here, do you want to see?"

Meghan nodded politely, and Trudy showed her several

features on the phone. "It captures even the tiniest details. It's been so fun to have something new to try, and I love playing with it. Again, though, Meghan, I am sorry I used it at the ball. I know I shouldn't have."

Meghan smiled. "It's all okay," she told Trudy. "I'm just glad I know that you are okay, Trudy. Let's consider this a fresh start; I'm ready to forget the rough last few weeks if you are?"

Trudy grinned. "Yes, I am," she replied to Meghan. "Being so angry hurts *me*, and I am ready to be back to my normal self."

The two women continued walking. They were on the outskirts of Sandy Bay, and Meghan squinted, recognizing a familiar figure who was walking their way. "Look," Meghan pointed. "It's Pamela. Why don't we say hello?"

The three women greeted each other. "Pamela," Meghan said. "Trudy is ready to start fresh this week. We can get back to normal at Truly Sweet."

Pamela's face was dark. "I don't know about normal," she responded in a quivering voice. "My mom just called; the police are at my house, and I have to go home. They're looking for me."

Meghan bit her lip. "Yeah, I know," she said. "I was actually going to escort Trudy into the station; Jack told me that the police are talking with everyone who was in the kitchen at the ball, and they want to interview the pair of you. It shouldn't be too difficult, though; as long as you answer their questions honestly, it will all be okay. They'll probably ask about your whereabouts before the ball, your feelings toward Paula, and some other questions about the night she died."

As the trio arrived at the police station, Meghan's stomach churned when she spotted the reporter in the trench coat who had shown up at the bakery. He waved at her, smiling wolfishly as he shoved a microphone in her face.

"Meghan Truman, can you say a few words on the investigation of Paula Brown's death? Is there a reason you are accompanying two of the police's suspects to the station?"

Meghan glared at the reporter. "You should have told me you were a reporter when you asked me questions in my bakery," she hissed.

The reporter smirked. "You should have been smart enough to figure that out."

Meghan gritted her teeth as she tried to push past the reporter. "Get out of our way. We are trying to get inside of the station, and you are blocking us from entering."

The reporter chuckled. "I'm not moving until you answer my questions. Now, Meghan, what can you tell us about Paula Brown's murder? I hear the police have declared her death to be a murder. Can you say more on the state of the investigation?"

Meghan's face was burning with anger, and as the reporter jabbed the microphone back into her face, Meghan tore it from his hands. She reared back and sent the microphone crashing down on the concrete steps of the police station.

"Hey! You cannot do that," the reporter exclaimed as he bent down to collect the pieces of his broken microphone. "I'll sue you for that. That's my private property, and you ruined it."

Just as Meghan opened her mouth to argue, a police officer walked out of the station. "Officer," the reporter pleaded. "This woman damaged my property. I would like to file a police report immediately."

The police officer looked between Meghan and the reporter, and then down at the pieces of the microphone that lay on the ground. "I didn't see anything," the officer replied, slicking back his hair and nodding kindly at Meghan. "Besides, I know Ms. Truman here would never hurt a fly, let along damage the property of a slimeball reporter like yourself."

The reporter frowned. "Excuse me?"

The officer narrowed his eyes. "That report you did on the local schools? It was demeaning for teachers; you suggested that Sandy Bay teachers don't care about their students. Guess what, buddy? My wife is a teacher, and you hurt her feelings with that trashy piece of journalism. My word here is that Meghan didn't touch you, or your microphone. Now, you all have a good day."

The officer strutted away, and Meghan flipped her hair behind her shoulder. "You heard him," she gloated to the reporter. "You have a good day."

As Meghan turned on her heel and marched into the station, Pamela turned to Trudy and whispered, in awe, "I've learned something today, Trudy: no one messes with Meghan Truman. She may be truly *sweet*, but she is also truly *fierce*."

The police station was bustling; Meghan saw dozens of people waiting to be interviewed, and the three women could not find a free chair amongst the crowd.

"Hey, those people were working in the kitchen with us," Pamela whispered to Meghan as she pointed to four mustached men. "They were part of Claude's team. There was another guy with them who was my age, and man, he was so cute."

Meghan laughed. "Pamela, you silly goose."

The three women sat down on the floor of the station. Suddenly, Jack emerged from his office, and Meghan perked up, shyly tucking her hair behind her ears and straightening her posture.

"With that look in your eyes, I'm going to guess that things are fine with you and Jack?" Trudy asked as she leaned against the wall.

"Yes," Meghan confirmed with a huge smile on her face. "We talked it all through, and it's all going to be okay."

Trudy grinned. "I'm so happy to hear that."

Jack approached the women, and Meghan stood up to plant a kiss on his cheek. Jack smiled sheepishly, and then he gave Meghan a sweet kiss on the lips.

"Gross!" Pamela screeched as Trudy shushed her.

"That's how I know you aren't ready for a French boyfriend," Meghan laughed.

Jack's face turned serious as he surveyed the busy hallway. "We have over a hundred people to interview," he whispered into Meghan's ear. "We reviewed some of the footage from the kitchen tapes, and we are likely still going to speak with Trudy and Pamela. Chief Nunan asked me to keep everyone corralled here, though, so if you could just stay a bit longer?"

Meghan nodded. "No problem. We'll keep ourselves entertained, right, ladies?"

Trudy smiled. "We can play around with my new phone camera. Pamela, I was showing Meghan my new toy earlier, but now I can show you. I have some cute pictures of you from the Governor's Ball. Do you want to see?"

Pamela grinned. "Yes! Cute candid pictures are my favorite; I want to post some online if they're super cute."

Jack kissed Meghan's forehead and walked back to his office. The three women settled back on the floor. Trudy removed her phone from her coat and began scrolling through her photos.

"This is a picture of you, Pamela," Trudy said as she showed Pamela the screen. "Look how cute you look in your Truly Sweet smock. Just adorable."

Meghan gestured at the screen. "I knew you both would look gorgeous in the smocks. What other photos do you have on there, Trudy? Any photos of me?"

"Well, you weren't in the kitchen, so probably not, but let me check," Trudy told Meghan. "There are some videos on here. Meghan, why don't you look? My eyes are starting to hurt from squinting at this tiny screen."

Trudy handed the phone to Meghan, and she began to thumb through the videos and images. She stopped when she saw a familiar face, smiling as she recalled her pleasant encounter with the subject.

"This is Donnie," Meghan exclaimed as she tilted the phone toward Pamela and Trudy. "He was Paula's assistant. I met him in the fruit market, and he was so kind. He wants to get into politics someday. We had a great chat. I bet he would like some of these candid photos. He looks so elegant in his outfit!"

Meghan flipped through several more candid shots of Donnie. "Ooooh, there's a video, too," Meghan told the women. "Oh, no…"

After pressing play, Meghan's heart began to pound. On the small screen of the camera, Meghan watched as Donnie reached into his pocket and retrieved something that looked like tablets. Meghan scrolled to the next video, where she saw Donnie look right, and then left, and then drop the tablets into a bowl of ice cream.

"Oh my goodness," Meghan whispered as she froze the image. "It was Donnie. Donnie poisoned Paula. Her own assistant poisoned her!"

Trudy grabbed the camera from Meghan and stared at the tiny video screen. "Let me see that," Trudy ordered.

"You're right," Trudy concluded, her eyes widening as the second video ended. "He did it. That man in my video poisoned the ice cream, and we have video evidence. Meghan, you need to take my camera to your sweetheart right now!"

Meghan stood up from her place on the floor. She sprinted down the hallway and burst into Jack's office. "Jack, I know who poisoned Paula. You can send these people home; Donnie, Paula's assistant, killed her, and I have video evidence."

"Is that so?"

Meghan nodded as Chief Nunan stepped into the room. "I heard what you said, Meghan," Chief Nunan told her. "Is the video on that phone?"

Meghan bobbed her head and gave the phone to Chief Nunan. "It's all on there, Chief Nunan. See for yourself."

Chief Nunan turned on the camera and watched the two videos. "Yes, you are right," Chief Nunan said as the second video ended. "We have enough evidence to arrest Donnie, Paula's assistant. Jack? I want you to spread the word: Donnie is now our primary suspect, and I have great reason to believe that he killed his employer. I want every officer and detective out on this guy, and I want him brought to me *immediately.*"

"All of this happened while I was on my yoga retreat?" Karen Denton laughed into the phone as Meghan strolled down the beach. "To think I missed the ball, a breakup, and a murder! I moved back to Sandy Bay for some peace and quiet, but it feels like peace and quiet is never quite the case..."

Meghan chuckled, happy to hear her dear friend's voice. Karen had been in Costa Rica for nearly two weeks, and Meghan could hardly wait to fill her in on all the events following the Governor's Ball.

"This is why you had to go find inner peace," Meghan joked. "You knew you couldn't find it here, so you had to go all the way to Costa Rica."

Karen giggled. "You caught me. Speaking of getting caught... tell me about how they caught that Donnie ding-dong. I can't believe he killed his own boss."

"I know," she agreed. "It's terrible. Jack and Chief Nunan dragged Donnie kicking and screaming out of the Governor's Mansion about an hour after I showed them the video. They found more poison in the Governor's kitchen, and it looks like Donnie was planning to kill the Governor, too."

"Good thing Trudy showed you that footage, or other innocent people would have died," Karen said. "Seriously, I just can't believe she caught it on film by accident. What are the odds?"

Meghan shivered as a gust of cold wind slapped her face. She zipped her long, purple coat higher up her neck and shuddered; she hated being cold, and despite loving her life in Sandy Bay, when it was chilly, Meghan ached for the mild Los Angeles weather that she had previously lived in.

"So did Jack tell you why Donnie did it?" Karen asked.

"Donnie confessed right away. He told Jack and Chief Nunan that Paula had undermined his political aspirations by reporting him to the Governor's compliance officer for not declaring a gift he had received while on official duty, and had threatened that she was going to ruin his chances at being elected to office someday."

Karen sighed. "I hope that buffoon knows now that he'll never be elected; he not only killed his boss, but he ruined his own life."

"He did," Meghan said. "He ruined his life, but thankfully, mine is back on track; Jack and I had dinner with his friend, Michelle, and I was able to apologize for being rude, and she even apologized for not thinking of my feelings. She and I probably won't ever be best friends, but at least we aren't enemies."

"That's good," Karen agreed. "It's never good to have an enemy. So... Jack? What's going on there? Are things okay?"

Despite the harsh winds biting at her skin, Meghan beamed. "We're okay, Karen. Actually, we are more than okay; when Jack and I were making up, he told me he loves me. I said it back to him, too. We are in love, and better than ever."

"That's wonderful news," Karen cooed as Meghan thought about her handsome boyfriend. "I'm over the moon that things have worked out. I wish I could have been in Sandy Bay to help you, but it sounds like you were able to fix things yourself."

Meghan grinned, thinking of how happy she was that she and Jack were back together, and imagining how she had stood up to the reporter outside of the police station. Meghan's heart warmed as she remembered the shy, meek girl she had been when she arrived in Sandy Bay, and compared that girl to the strong, resilient woman she was now.

"I've been learning to stand up for myself, Karen," Meghan informed her friend. "I feel like I learn something new every single day here in Sandy Bay. Even the bad days have given me valuable lessons, and I can honestly say, without hesitation, that no matter the challenges, it is truly sweet to be in Sandy Bay with all of my friends and my *loved* ones!"

The End

THANK YOU!

Thank you for reading these three stories in the Sandy Bay Cozy Mystery series. I really hope you enjoyed reading it as much as I had writing it!

If you have a minute, please consider leaving a review on Amazon.

It doesn't matter how long or short it is as other cozy mystery readers will find value in what you liked about this book.

Many thanks in advance for your support!

ALSO BY AMBER CREWES

The Sandy Bay Cozy Mystery Series

Printed in Great Britain
by Amazon